LOGAN'S LOVE:
War Angels MC

Table of Contents

CHAPTER 1

Lo

We were sitting in the clubhouse for once having a quiet day. Friday afternoons for us were usually pretty busy but we weren't complaining about the lack of work. I had finished all the paperwork for the garage where we fixed and built custom motorcycles as well as some small engine repair.

Our garage bays were still full but not with anything pressing. Most of our customers had left for May Long weekend to go camping and for the first time in the five years I had lived in this little town the weather was cooperating with the vacationers.

I had just sat down at one of the tables in the main room of the club house with my VP and a couple of beers when we heard a vehicle pull up outside and a door slam.

"I guess that's the end of our quiet day." Axle said, taking a long pull on his bottle. He had no idea just how right he was. Axle had been my VP since we started the War Angels MC Club.

He had fought by my side in Iraq and Afghanistan as well as many other places we weren't allowed to mention and he had vowed to be at my side to the end. It was a promise we had made each other. When we both had retired from the Special Forces branch of the Canadian Armed Forces neither of us were of sound mind or body.

We had seen too many atrocities and horrifying things to ever be normal again. We had lost our brothers and sisters in combat in ways that cannot be unseen.

"Hello, I'm looking for Logan Winters, is he here today?" I heard the voice at the front door of the club where one of our men was standing guard.

We never expected trouble, but it's always nice to have someone on the lookout for a heads up and honestly it had become habit for so many of us to need the extra warning should trouble come knocking. I didn't hear what Hammer said but the low rumble of his gravelly voice sounded positive.

"Would I be able to see him?" The woman asked and the sound of her voice caught my attention. It was deeper, almost husky.

Again we heard the rasp of Hammer's voice and waited patiently for the fireworks. Hammer's voice box had been damaged in an IED attack overseas and he was often difficult to understand but that hadn't dampened his wicked and often inappropriate, sense of humor. I could just imagine the things he was telling this unknown woman.

"Pardon me?!?" That was the shrill answer that was my reward for my patience.

"This is gonna be good." Axle chuckled beside me, holding his empty beer bottle above his head, signaling the prospect at the bar for another.

"Prez?" The prospect asked, holding a full bottle up in question.

"Yup." I grunted, not taking my eyes off the door.

"You want me to do what to get inside?" Axle snorted beside me, rightly guessing that Hammer had propositioned the woman at the door. Again Hammer rumbled something and I could tell the answering growl was not from him and it was not a happy sound. "How about this, how about instead of me sucking your pencil dick I shove it so far up your ass you taste your own jizz for a while? Now get the fuck out of my way, I have business with Logan Winters."

"Prez, you pissed any bitches off lately? I mean more than usual?" Axle asked, keeping his eyes on the door as it opened and a stunned but laughing Hammer pointed the stranger to our table.

"Not since Demon's funeral and that cop that questioned us all." I replied, mentioning an older brother we had lost a few weeks ago in a lay down.

He had gotten himself into some shit we didn't support, we weren't a 1%ers club and we didn't deal in drugs, women or guns but Demon had gotten hooked in with a small time drug dealer trying to be big time and got caught in a raid.

Demon had tried to get away but after a rather high speed chase with the cops he had turned his bike in a sharp curve and lost his tires on some gravel. He had been going too fast to control his fall or his slide and he wasn't wearing a helmet.

As the unknown woman stepped past Hammer and blocked the sun shining through the door my breath caught in my chest. The sun shone around her and the shadows blocked her face but her figure was full and sleek.

She paused in the door, turning her chin just enough to listen to what Hammer whispered in her ear, visibly scoffed then continued walking across the room. When she stopped at our table she cocked her hip and stood akimbo glaring from Axle to me, definitely not impressed with what she saw.

"Which one of you is Logan Winters?" She demanded, her forehead creasing in a scowl.

"Who wants to know?" Axle asked lazily. I could tell by the way Axle gripped his beer bottle that he was anything but leisurely or lazy at this point.

I was also more than happy to let him speak for me, at least until we knew who this woman was and what she wanted. She sized Axle up for a moment then turned her attention to me and completely ignored him. Her gaze was astute and she was obviously no dummy.

"Mr. Winters." She began, relaxing her stance slightly and pulling something out of the back pocket of her jeans. If I were a weaker man my mouth would've started to water at the sight of those tight jeans pulled across her rounded hips. "Do you know this man?" She demanded, tossing the paper she pulled from her pocket onto the table in front of me.

My gaze flicked from her face to the paper and recognized a picture of Demon from shortly before he died. He was facing away from the camera but his cut was clear with our club patch and rockers with our name and his road name on it.

"I might." I replied, tipping my bottle back. This woman was smart and she could probably tell if I lied to her.

"Well, Mr. Winters –"

"Lo."

"Pardon me?"

"My name is Lo, not Mr. Winters."

"Uh huh, Lo, do you know the gentleman in the picture or not?"

"Miss, you just walked in here rather snarky demanding answers to questions and we don't even know your name." Axle said, cocking an eyebrow.

"Mr. – Lo, is there somewhere we can speak privately?" The woman asked, barely sparing Axle a glance.

"Nope," I replied, taking a sip of my beer and relaxing my posture even more. "Axle is my VP, anything you have to tell me you tell him." Axle smirked at the look of consternation on her pretty face.

It wasn't a beautiful face. Her cheeks were a bit too full, her nose slightly off center and her bottom lip too full for her top one, but her eyes were all full dark lashes and sparkling green and gold in a blanket of chocolate, her skin was like porcelain and would probably feel like silk under my hands.

Where the fuck did that come from? Suddenly I'm a fucking poet.

"Fine, that man has disappeared!" She declared pointing at the picture. "His 14 year old daughter is living at my parents' house scared out of her mind. Her mother died just over a year ago and now her father has disappeared. If you know that man, or what may have happened to him I need to know."

"Well darlin'," Axle drawled, "That there is a need to know info and it doesn't seem to be that you need to know, specially since you just lied to us."

"Pardon me?" She demanded, turning her glare back to Axle. "I didn't lie to you jackass! The 14 year old girl my son brought home from school half-starved and freezing is proof of that."

"No, all that is proof of is that your kid brings home strays. That doesn't prove any connections to this club." Axle reasoned. Obviously this woman was way past reasoning with.

"Right," She sneered at Axle before turning her attention back to me. "Are you going to answer me or not? Do you know this man, and if so, do you know where I might find him?"

"I know him." I replied slowly. "And where you can find him, but he ain't talkin'."

"What the fuck is that supposed to mean?"

"He's dead."

"I'm sorry, what?"

"He was killed 3 weeks ago when he crashed his bike." I said, taking a pull on my beer.

"Oh for fuck sakes," She said, pushing her bangs off her forehead and looking at the ground before directing her gaze to the roof. "Shit! Well, thanks for nothing." She started to spin on her heel to leave but I had caught a look in her eye I didn't like.

"You got a problem with what you see here lady?" I demanded before she could stalk away.

"Do I have a problem with two grown men drinking beer in a dinghy bar at one in the afternoon? Nope, not at all, I don't have a problem with the ranch out back of here where I'm sure you work very hard cleaning horse stalls and taking care of your animals that look very healthy. I don't have a problem with the very nice motorbikes out front or the obvious care and time you all take keeping them so nice and running. I don't actually have a problem with two grown men drinking beer in the middle of a work day at one in the afternoon.

"None of that even registers on my give-a-shit-meter. What I do have a problem with is the obvious lack of compassion for a child who has lost both her mother and father in less than a year and is relying on the charity of practical strangers. But hey, drink your fucking beer, ride your fucking horses, work on your pretty fucking bikes and go on with your fuck-tastic lives. I need to go and figure out how I'm going to get custody of a child when I already have five of my own and one income, but thanks so fucking much for your help, it was overwhelming." She turned to leave and stopped short when she found she had drawn a crowd. "Fuck."

We sat and watched her shove her way through the crowd and stomp out of the clubhouse, letting the door slam behind her. A few of the men watched her go but most kept their eyes on me, waiting for . . . something.

"Wow, she's . . . something." Axle said, finishing off his beer. "Well, I'm going to get a shower."

"What's that about, Prez?" Hammer rasped, sitting in the chair Axle just vacated.

"Demon," was my only reply. How did we not know the man had a kid, or that she was living here with him? "Fuck. Anyone know about this kid?"

Hammer shook his head no, but looked around the room and the small pockets of men laughing, talking, playing pool, and basically just shootin' the shit. There were about twenty guys here right now, about half our numbers. The other half of our guys worked either at our construction business, or at their own jobs.

All of our men were vets and had served in some way in the Canadian Armed Forces. We were all connected in some way, I didn't personally serve with each and every man in the club but I served with a brother who served with a brother. Not all of us were Special Forces and even fewer of us were JTF 2.

Joint Task Force, CAFs version of the Navy SEALs only where the SEALs were getting a lot of press lately, JTF was still flying below the radar somewhat. No one knew you were in JTF and no one talked about JTF. It was like Fight Club, the first rule about fight club is you don't talk about fight club.

"You catch that broad's name?" Hammer asked, scanning the room. I shook my head no and waited for him to continue. "You see her jacket?" I looked at my brother expectantly; he obviously had noticed something I hadn't. "Catholic school emblem on the top left. She mentioned kids?" I nodded realizing I had totally missed a very important clue. "Guess you were too busy staring at that ass, eh?" Hammer chuckled when I grunted then slammed back his whisky.

"Seether!" I hollered across the clubhouse. I needed to find out who that woman was and what the hell was going on with Demon before he died. Seether was our tech guru and if anyone could figure this shit out it was him.

CHAPTER 2

Alana

What the hell was I going to do now? I had found Chelle's dad but he was dead. He certainly wasn't going to help and neither was that club. How the hell was I going to raise 6 kids on a single income?

Six years after my husband had died leaving me with our five kids to raise alone, one of whom was deaf, I was taking on another child and more responsibility that I didn't need. Unfortunately for me, but fortunately for Chelle, what I needed wasn't at the top of my give a shit list. What I needed from any given situation often rated far at the bottom of the list if it had anything at all to do with my kids.

My oldest was fifteen and probably missed his dad more than any of the others. Nate was only nine when Mike, my husband, was killed and definitely needed his dad on so many levels. Hence the reason we moved closer to my parents. If my kids couldn't have their dad they could at least have mine. Caleb, Cal, needed his dad but in different ways.

Nate was sensitive and artistic, needed extra help in school. Cal was a sweet boy at 13 who always wanted to try new things and excelled at everything he tried. Jack was 11 and a math-magician/jock. The boy had never met a sport or a math problem he couldn't conquer. Link was my silly boy at 9. Really he was too smart for his own good but like his father he needed a really good reason to get excited about something and school didn't cut it.

Drew, my baby was 5 and deaf. As soon as we could when he was a baby we had him fitted with a cochlear implant but we all learned sign language. The deaf community was culture all its own and I was not about to take away a choice at belonging anywhere and everywhere for my boy.

Now with Nate's friend Michelle in our lives our day to day just got a bit more exciting. I was used to being the only female in the house at any given time. Chelle, while super quiet and shy was another aspect we would have to get used to. For better or worse she was ours now.

"Mom, I don't know what I'm going to do." I said to my mom as I chopped vegetables for supper. It had been four days since I had found Chelle's dad, or rather I didn't find her dad, but at least now I knew where he was and so did she. She was still at my parent's house. She hadn't gone to school today and was still trying to decide whether or not she wanted to know more than we did now. She had an appointment with a counsellor tomorrow to help her process the last horrible year of her life.

"You're going to do what you always do." My mom said from behind me at the stove where she was stirring meat sauce for spaghetti. "You're going to take on too much, get way too stressed over something that you shouldn't have to deal with in the first place, then you'll rework the entire situation and everything will turn out exactly how it's meant to. You know you'll stress out then realize you need to let go and let God, you'll start praying and God will guide you."

"Shit, you're so right."

"Watch your language, the kids are home."

"Mom, the only kid who's close enough to hear me is deaf." I replied, chuckling. Drew was at the kitchen table on the other side of the kitchen counter colouring a math worksheet his kindergarten teacher sent home for him to do for fun. Insane that a woman who couldn't do simple algebra until the age of 25 would have four out of five kids who loved math. I swear God was standing up at the pearly gates with St. Peter laughing His ass off.

"Practice, if you swear when the deaf kid is around then you'll swear when the hearing kids are around." My mother was always so smart with all the answers.

"All right, are you staying for supper?"

"No sweetie, your dad is picking me up when he drops Nate and Cal off. They should be here any minute." Sure enough my mother's apparent ESP had kicked in and my two oldest boys rushed into the house. Cal sweaty from baseball practice and Nate covered in sawdust from working with his grandfather on a new set of shelves he was building for his room.

My dad had always been handy, but more in a put-up-dry-wall sort of way. Now that Nate had found his calling in carpentry my dad really had to step up his game, they took classes together at the local technical college.

"Mom, what's for supper?" Cal called as he walked in the kitchen.

"Nothing until you two shower, you stink I can smell you from here." I called back to him smiling as he rolled his eyes.

"Well, I'll see you tomorrow dear." My mom said as she washed her hands and wiped them on a towel. "Goodbye Drew." She said as she signed to my little boy. He looked up at her and smiled then waved. "Alana, there's a gentleman at your door, dear." She called back as she walked out the door.

There was a gentleman at my door? Odd, all of my neighbours were women, and most of them single moms living with their kids in our low income housing complex. The places weren't new but they were in pretty good condition and the yards were a decent size.

"Hello?" I called, wiping my hands on the same towel my mom used as I followed her to the front door, only to get the shock of my life! "Oh! Mr. Winters!"

"Lo."

"Right, Lo. How did you find me? And what are you doing at my house?" I demanded as Jack walked up behind me.

"Everything all right mom?" He asked, eyeing this stranger in leather.

"Uh, yeah Hun. Can you go and get supper for you and your younger brothers? Nate and Cal can get theirs when they come down." I replied distractedly.

"What about you?"

"Um, I'll get mine in a bit, go ahead sweetie."

"Do you have a minute to talk?" Lo asked, shoving his hands into the pockets of his worn jeans.

"Uh, sure, outside ok? I have a feeling whatever it is you need to tell me my boys don't need to hear it." Lo shrugged and stepped back so I could move outside.

We stood staring at each other for a minute before we both opened our mouths to speak at the same time, me to ask again what the hell he was doing on my front step and him to comment on how interesting he found my Spotify list. I took a breath to answer just as 3 Doors Down finished and Bryan Adams started. I really didn't have an answer for my eclectic taste in music so I just shrugged.

"I looked into Demon." Lo said watching my face for a reaction. "You were right."

"And?" I said when he stopped there.

"Yes he has a daughter, yes she is fourteen and yes for the last eight months she has been living with him." He sighed.

"You're not telling me anything I didn't already know, Lo. I've even been to the crappy shack he called a house. From what I could tell of your clubhouse and surrounding ranch the other day, not to mention all the motorcycles scattered around the lot I would say you all have a bit of money. I researched you all as well. I know all the charity work and such you do around here."

"Your point?"

"My point, is that if you all are relatively well off then why did Demon have his teenage daughter living in a dive in one of the worst parts of town? And then going to the most expensive private school in town?"

Lo pulled his hands out of his pockets and rubbed his face, pushing his dark hair back as he tipped his head to look at the sky and place his hands on his hips.

"I can't answer all of those questions. And I'm not even sure I should if I could. I can tell you the what, but not necessarily the why. Look, it's getting fucking hot out here. Is there somewhere we can go with air conditioning and sit down?" I looked back behind me at my front door then back at Lo.

"Let me get my kids figured out and I'll meet you at the Tim's at the bottom of the hill." I said, turning and walking away without waiting for an answer. I was just about to close the door when I heard his reply.

"I won't wait long." He said, "Either you want your answers or not." I didn't answer, just looked into his eyes and shut the door. I stayed there at the door until I heard his heavy boots stomp away and his motorbike start up and roar away.

"Who's that?" Nate demanded behind me.

"Oh!" I jumped and spun around. "You scared the crap out of me Nate." He said nothing just watched me expectantly. "That was Chelle's dad's boss. He has some answers about Demon. I'm gonna meet him at the Tim Horton's at the bottom of the hill. You go get your supper, watch the boys for me for an hour?"

"I should go with you, he's not safe."

"I'm sure he's not." I responded chuckling. "That's why I'm meeting him at a very busy restaurant and not letting him anywhere near my kids. Please, do as I ask. I won't be long, I promise." Nate sighed and shook his head. My 15 year old baby boy was turning into a man right in front of my eyes. It just about made me tear up.

"I don't trust him." Nate said but gave in. I didn't trust him either, not only was Lo dangerous looking he was also too handsome for my own good.

CHAPTER 3

Lo

I sat at the coffee shop for five minutes before Alana walked in. I had gotten us both black coffees with cream and sugar on the side and sat in a quiet corner where I could see the door. As soon as she walked in I stood up and signaled to her. I watched her walk over, again admiring the way she moved.

She was wearing jeans again but had lost the jacket in favour of a light sweater. When she stood in front of me I noticed for the first time how tall she was.

I had thought she was around average height, and since I was half-way over six feet I didn't think much of it when she barely came to my shoulder, but standing with her now I realized she was a few inches taller than average.

She was also not small, this woman was built like an athlete and after five kids I could tell she would never be a waif. Her hair was down today when the last time I saw her it had been pulled back into a fancy braid. Now it fell past her shoulders in thick curls coloured to look like an oil spill.

"I grabbed you a coffee." I said, motioning for her to sit. "Wasn't sure how you took it so I grabbed cream and sugar on the side."

"Black is fine, thanks." She said, taking a sip. "So, please tell me first how you found me."

"Your jacket," I said after a second watching her tuck her hair behind her ear. She looked up at me quickly and frowned. "The day you came to the clubhouse you were wearing a jacket with an emblem from one of the local schools. I had my tech guy go on the school's website and see what was there. We didn't think we would find you were part of the staff but it sure made our lives easier."

"Shit." She said pushing back to sit back in her chair.

"I have to say you're not what I would expect of someone working at a Catholic school." I said, smirking.

"Meaning?"

"Meaning, not too many nuns have rainbow hair, five kids and swear like a sailor."

"Good thing I'm not a nun then, eh?" She said, taking another sip of her coffee. "So, tell me what you learned about Demon."

I watched her for another minute, trying to figure out what she was thinking. She was obviously uncomfortable but I couldn't tell why or if it was just me.

"Turns out I didn't know Demon as well as I thought I did." I replied, blowing out a breath.

"No shit." She scoffed, playing with a sugar packet.

"Not too many men who can hide a child and a house from men he works alongside day in and day out. We didn't know about the house because he had his own room at the clubhouse and spent more nights there than not, easy enough to miss. A kid though, he had to really make an effort to hide her."

"Why would he hide her from you?" Alana asked, finally really looking me in the eye. Damn I could drown in her eyes. "I mean, you're not dangerous are you?"

"You obviously think I am since you wouldn't let me in your house or near your kids."

"Mr. Winters, every man is a danger to my kids until they have proven to me that they are not. Given that you are the president of a motorcycle club and one of your members was killed running from the police after a drug raid, I will definitely put you on the danger list when it comes to my kids and you will more than likely stay there."

"Hmm, smart and beautiful," I mumbled and took a drink of my own coffee.

"Oh please." She rolled her eyes at me and shook her head.

"And it's Lo; please don't call me Mr. Winters."

"Feeling your age?" She retorted. I laughed out loud at that, throwing my head back as I did.

"I'm hardly that old."

"Old enough to be trying to avoid it apparently," She replied. "So, what else can you tell me about Demon?"

"Nothing really, most everything else is club business, but we did find a letter when we went through his stuff. After he died we just put all of his stuff in a couple of boxes and into storage. His clothes and other things were donated and papers and whatever put away to go through when Seether had time."

"Seether?"

"Our tech guy, he's an all-around financial computer genius, does all that stuff for the club and our businesses, but don't tell him I said he was a genius, his head's already big enough. Anyway, after you left that day I had him find you and then put everything else he was doing on the back burner and go through Demon's stuff. Very interesting guy, our Demon."

"I'm sure." She agreed. "What did . . . Seether, find in Demon's papers?"

"Custody papers for the girl – "

"Her name is Michelle, or Chelle."

"Sorry, we found custody papers for Michelle, info on her mom, how she died and how she lived before that, where they were living and a letter from Demon to me asking me to look after his daughter if anything happened to him."

"No." Alana exclaimed. "Not a chance!" She grabbed her purse and started to get up, almost knocking her coffee over.

"Now wait a minute." I said grabbing her hand.

"No, no minutes. You are not getting Chelle."

"I don't want her." I said roughly. "The letter only asked me to look after her, far as I can tell she's taken care of with you." She calmed quickly but didn't take her hand from mine.

"Thank you." She whispered. "We've kind of gotten attached to her. My mom and dad really like having a granddaughter."

"Look, can you tell me how Michelle came to be living with y'all?"

"Nate, my oldest goes to the same school as her, where I work. They have a couple of classes together even though she's a year younger than he is. He would see her in the cafeteria all the time and at first she seemed fine. He's kind of a softy and has been the new kid at school enough times to know it sucks so when she first moved here in September he kept an eye on her and chatted with her once in a while." Alana sighed and looked around the restaurant.

"By November they were good friends and spent a lot of time together in and out of school. Not romantically, Nate swears he doesn't see her that way but he's a fifteen year old boy, we'll see how long it takes for that to change." She shrugged, obviously knowing her son better than anyone.

I snorted, knowing she was probably right. She obviously knew her kid pretty damn good.

"Anyway, Chelle always had lunch and clean clothes, if not new ones and said when she had moved here she had never met her dad before but for the most part he was nice to her. They didn't spend any time together and more often than not she never saw him. She'd wake up in the morning to find a few hundred dollars on the kitchen counter for groceries or whatever every couple of days and she would use what she needed then leave the rest in a jar.

"She said her dad never touched the money in the jar and after he disappeared she went through it pretty quick. He had always kept the bills paid, heat on, water running, TV and internet working, lights on but Chelle said he had disappeared long before he actually died. Like I said, the money ran out fast."

"How long was he missing before he died?" I demanded.

CHAPTER 4

Alana

Lo was getting angry. Shit. He was kind of scary when he was smiling and happy. Lo angry was far past my holy shit limit.

"How long?" He demanded again when I didn't answer right away.

"Well, he died three weeks ago right?" I said, trying to gather my thoughts. Lo nodded, waiting for me to continue. "Um, Nate came to me right after Christmas and told me Chelle had no food at home and was freezing?"

"What?" I don't think anyone had ever yelled at me like that before, but I'm pretty sure I was just bellowed at.

"From what Nate and Chelle told me the last time she saw her dad was right after the New Year, maybe the fourth of January? She ran out of money by the middle of March and once Demon died the power and everything in his house was cut off. No one knew about her so there was no reason to keep the heat or anything on. She moved in with my parents about two weeks ago. She was trying to go it alone with what she had but then the money ran out and without heat or water she couldn't stay in that house."

"Fuck!" Lo shoved his chair back, almost knocking it over and stormed out of the restaurant. I watched wide eyed as he slammed out the door then felt like I was being watched. As I turned back to the rest of the restaurant I found many pairs of eyes on me.

"Um, s-sorry," I said. I quickly gathered our empty coffee cups, dumped them in the garbage and followed Lo much more sedately outside. "I thought you wanted to talk where it was air conditioned, how'd we end up back outside? We could've stayed in my yard and not drank bad coffee or made a spectacle."

"Fuck," he chuckled, shaking his head, pushing his hands onto his hips. "You're something else, aren't you?"

"So I've been told." I shrugged. "Look, I'm sure you're super trustworthy and all, but how legal is this letter of Demon's asking you to look out for Chelle?"

"I'll show it to you. Looks like it's notarized though."

"Awesome, your ecru coloured friend may not have been operating completely outside of the law."

"What, ecru? What the fuck is ecru?"

"Not white, more of a beige. As in his ass wasn't lily white and pure."

"You know, I swear a lot. I'm not gonna lie, but I know I swear a lot more when you're around." Lo shook his head and chuckled.

"Right, so what's our next move?"

"Demon might have been an SOB, but he did set up a savings account for Michelle and there's a lot of money in there. I'll make sure you get it."

"Nope, I don't want Chelle's money. If the account is in her name then leave it there and she can have it when she needs it. She hasn't said much about her future but I know she thinks about it and she's going to need that money."

"You are currently raising five boys on your own –"

"Am not!"

"Ok, yes, your parents help you out. How often do you take their money?"

"Point to Lo."

"Yeah, so you're raising five boys on your own. One kid is not cheap, I may not be a parent but I was once a teenaged boy and I know I was expensive. Clothing, feeding, sports other shit kids do. I also know you make decent money, but it's not much. You choose to work for the private school board that cannot pay you nearly as much as the public board, and now you're taking on the care of yet another teenager."

"Girls don't eat as much as boys. She's really quite cheap." I shrugged. "And for the most part my boys wear hand me downs."

"Uh huh and how often do clothes get to number four in line before they're destroyed? Not to mention number five? And a girl can't really wear boys' hand me downs. Does Michelle wear make-up? Do shit with her hair? She does eat, right? Does she do extra-curricular stuff? Yeah, so she's not free."

"What's your point?"

Lo sighed as though he knew he was about to have a battle on his hands. What can I say? I'm difficult.

"Demon was a brother, the club has money-"

"No-"

"Hear me out!" Lo growled, cutting my arguments down with a look. "The club has money and it's all legal. Besides the shop, we have the ranch which is sort of a hobby ranch. It doesn't make a lot of money because of overhead, but we also have a very busy, very lucrative construction business. All of our members get a cut of the profits and we have managed to work out a pension plan of sorts for employees.

"Demon worked for each of the three businesses at any given

time. He never used his money, always stashed it in the bank. Because Demon was one of ours so is Michelle and Demon asked me specifically to look out for her. I will be more than happy to sign custody or guardianship or whatever over to you legally but please let us help out financially."

I stared at this man in front of me, wondering if there was a catch. There had to be, right? Perhaps full disclosure was needed.

"You know, the school isn't my only source of income. I actually make pretty good money on the side. It's just that most of it is tied up in royalties and such."

"Royalties?"

"Um, yeah, I write romance novels, I do a little art that I sell, mostly people pay me to draw up their tattoos but I also sell a painting here and there."

"You're a tattoo artist on the side?"

"No, I don't do the actual ink. I'm not steady enough for that. Mostly people come to me and tell me what they want or what they want to represent and I take notes or whatever and then draw what they want and they pay me for it. That's all."

"Would you do one for me?"

"Umm sure?"

"Are you asking?"

"No, Lo, I can do one for you, but that means spending more time together."

"And, you don't like me enough to have another coffee with me?"

"No, I like you just fine I guess-"

"You guess?"

"Well, I did just meet you. We've had two conversations and both included a lot of the 'F' word and a lot of anger. Are you sure you want to spend more time with me? We tend to make each other angry."

"No we don't." Lo said as though what I said exasperated him. "You don't make me angry it just seems our conversations so far have revolved around really maddening topics."

"All right, I'll draw you a tattoo. Any ideas what you'd like? Or where you want to put it? Do you want colour? Outline? Filled in? Shaded?"

"I thought we were going to discuss this another time over coffee?"

"We are, I just would like some idea of what you'd like first."

"Is there going to be a questionnaire? Do I need to fill out a survey?" Lo asked, crossing his massive arms over his chest. How did I not notice before how completely muscled and ripped this guy was?

"Huh," I said, suddenly totally distracted by the man in front of me. "Um, that's not a bad idea, but no, or at least not really. I have certain questions that I ask that may lead to other questions based on your answers but no, nothing formal."

"Then perhaps we should do this over lunch." Lo said tilting his head at me. "I'll pick you up Saturday at 11." He announced then turned towards his bike.

"Wait! What?" Before I could ask anything else he swung his leg over his bike and cranked it. It roared to life growled as he sat on it putting on his helmet. I saw him smile as he did up the chin strap and pushed opaque sunglasses over his eyes. "I can't ride that!" I yelled over the rumble of the bike.

"Don't worry, I'll bring the truck."

"I'd much rather meet you somewhere."

"Too bad." And with that he was gone and I stood in the parking lot of the Tim Horton's completely dumb struck by the last ten minutes.

"This is ridiculous." I mumbled to myself Saturday morning as I shuffled through the clothes hanging in my closet. This was not a date! What did it matter what I wore?

This was a jeans and leather wearing biker, Lo didn't care what I wore. And it's not like I was trying to impress him, so what if he was the hottest man I had ever seen in my life, that didn't mean anything right?

"Jeans and a T-shirt it is!" In the end it was dark skinny jeans that made my ass look amazing and sucked my gut in and a flowered tank top with an asymmetrical sweater with strategic cut outs. And ballet flats. Lo might be a good eight to ten inches taller than me but I was going for comfort. Who was I kidding, I was totally dressing to impress him.

"Mom!" Cal called from the top of the stairs. When we had moved into this condo we didn't have a lot of options, its three floors with three bedrooms but really still not a lot of space for six people. The four bigger boys share two bedrooms upstairs and the smaller room is an office/craft room.

There aren't really any bedrooms in the basement and it's not completely finished, but I wanted Drew to be close in case there was an emergency that he couldn't hear in his sleep. We put up a few curtains for privacy but really we were spread out over half the basement. The other half was a playroom/TV space. It worked for us.

"There's a guy here for you!"

"Cal, that's kind of rude! Can you please stop yelling at your mother across the house?" I called back to him.

"But you just yelled up the stairs at me!" He replied, hoping to trap me.

"And it was rude wasn't it?" Oh motherhood. I reached the top step just in time to see Cal roll his eyes so I ruffled his hair and playfully shoved him out of the way. "I'll be right back, I just have to grab a few things from my office." I told Lo, not stopping to get a good look at him, like I needed more of a distraction.

He didn't answer me so I rushed up the stairs and grabbed a few art pencils and a sketch book that would fit into my purse. When I got back to the main floor I found Lo and Drew having a staring contest. Or at least that's what it looked like.

"He's not wearing his hearing aids again." Jack said, smirking at Lo.

"Huh, apparently I'm a horrible parent because we now have further proof that my kids are little shits." I said shaking my head.

My four older boys laughed and disappeared throughout the house. I watched Drew watch Lo for a few more minutes before I decided to put Lo out of his misery. Stomping my foot hard enough of the floor to get my son's attention I waited for him to turn to me.

"You're being rude." I said out loud as I signed to Drew.

"I'm not, Mama." Drew signed quickly, shaking his head vigorously.

"You are." I translated as I signed. *"You're not translating what you're signing. How do you know Mr. Winters knows sign?"*

"I asked, he does." Drew replied as though to say duh, then turned back to Lo. *"Bye Lo!"* he signed then ran off to join his brothers.

"Cute kid." Lo said, smirking at me.

"I didn't know you knew ASL." I said dumbfounded staring at this hulk of a man who just won over the heart of my deaf son. Logan Winters was too good looking for his own good.

Thick dark chestnut coloured hair that was longer on top then the sides and back framed his chiseled features and strong jaw, but it was his eyes that killed me. A deep gray that I had seen flash darker the other night when he was angry.

His nose was strong and perfect and his lips almost made me start to drool. His deep voice broke me out of my perusal of his face with a dark chuckle.

"You don't know a lot about me. Guess this lunch is a good idea, eh?"

"Huh. You ready?" Without waiting for an answer I brushed passed him and walked out the door, hoping to hide the blush creeping up my cheeks at being caught staring. He chuckled and followed, closing the door behind him.

CHAPTER 5

Lo

The drive to the restaurant was quick and quiet. While our town was considered a city it still wasn't very big. We ended up at Moxies which was just fine with me. Good food and they wouldn't kick us out if we stayed longer than our meal lasted. Once we were seated and had ordered I decided to ask the questions I wanted answered first.

"Your youngest: he born deaf?"

"Yup, I was a little older when he was born and my pregnancy was pretty stressful. The doctors don't know if that has anything to do with Drew being deaf or if it was just happenstance, but we accepted it and moved on."

"We, your husband still around then?"

"Hmmm, nope," She said quietly, getting a far off look in her eyes. "He died right before I found out I was pregnant; hence the stressful pregnancy." She shrugged as though it didn't matter but I could tell it definitely did.

"How old is Drew? Six?"

"Five." Alana replied.

"You've been alone for over six years? Most of that time with five kids? Shit, that sucks."

"It did, it does. Life has gotten better, both with us moving here and the boys getting older. Time may not heal all wounds but it does help them hurt less."

"You still miss him?" I asked, taking a drink from my beer. Yes, beer. I'm sure Alana loved that, drinking beer in the middle of the day.

"Of course, I always will, but like I said, it gets easier. So," she said, changing the subject. "What were you thinking of for your tattoo?"

"I wasn't," I smirked, "I just needed an excuse to see you. And you look amazing today."

"Oh please, I look amazing every day." She smiled coyly. "Wasn't Demon's letter and the legal crap enough of an excuse to see me again?"

"Sure, but not nearly as much fun." At that point the waitress came back with our food so conversation stalled a bit while we ate. "Honestly though, I would like to see your art. I'm always open to new ink, kind of addicted to it now."

"I suppose there are worse things to be addicted to." Alana laughed. "I personally love my ink."

"You have tatts?" I demanded. "I gotta see this. How many? Where are they? What are they?"

"Ha! You think bikers have the market on ink cornered?" She asked wiping her hands on her napkin. "I have four. One is a maple leaf in a volleyball, another a Celtic cross and another, a stylized crucifix all in places that are not easily exposed. The last is the only one with colour and it's on the middle of my back. Flowers and symbols for my boys, guess I'll have to add something for Chelle now, eh?"

"I'd love to see them. How difficult to expose are they?" I

smirked, hoping they were all very difficult to uncover in public and that she'd allow me to take her somewhere private and do some exposing of other things as well.

"Not that difficult, but definitely covered by clothes, even my bathing suit. And no, you can't see them . . . yet." She said looking at me through her eyelashes.

"Ms. Alana Martin, are you teasing me? Flirting with me?"

"Nah," she said, shaking her head. "I'm far too old to tease or flirt." I threw my head back and laughed harder than I had laughed in a very long time.

"Please," I mocked, "You're so old, can't be more than 35!"

"Oh stop, shooting low on purpose. I'm over 40." She replied shaking her head.

"Me too," I shrugged

"Can I get you anything else?" The waitress asked, stopping again at our table. Her eyes were glued to me but I could only stare at Alana.

"Not for me, you babe, you want dessert or something?"

"No, Lo, I'm good."

"Just the check," I said, flicking my gaze up to the girl standing far too close to me and getting a good look at her overabundance of cleavage. When the check arrived it came with a phone number for Candy scrawled at the bottom. I don't know why, but I instantly saw red. "Alana babe, wait for me by the door, yeah? I'll be right there."

"All right, Lo."

"Seriously?" I demanded angrily of the waitress. "I'm here with my woman and you think you should give me your number? I'm old enough to be your father." I tossed a few bills on the counter and walked out shaking my head.

"Don't be too mad at her Lo, you are pretty hot, even for an old man." Alana smirked when I was standing beside her.

I couldn't help myself, I stopped and stared at her as she walked away then laughed my ass off. She stopped a few feet away and looked at me expectantly.

"Old man?" I demanded.

"Well, you did say you were over 40, and my kids tell me that's old." She shrugged and turned to walk away again but I saw the flick of a smile on her lips.

"Pretty hot?"

"Don't push it, Lo." She called back, shaking her head. "Besides, who said I was your woman?"

"Oh just wait," I said under my breath. "You will be."

The drive back to Alana's house was much less quiet than the ride to the restaurant. We didn't talk about anything of consequence but I did learn a few more things about her. Like she loved music and had very eclectic tastes, listening to anything from Metallica and Nickelback to REM and Ed Sheeran.

The only kind of music she really didn't like was rap. Fine by me, what little I could understand of it I had gotten enough of in Afghanistan and these guys got it all wrong anyway. When we worked in the garage we listened to a wide variety of music, it just depended on which of the guys was in the shop first.

Alana talked a little about her writing, too. She said the music helped with that as well. She said it was really hard to write a big bad biker (for instance) if she was listening to Bruno Mars.

She talked a little about her boys and then jumped to her parents and her siblings. I felt they were a topic that was off limits until we got to know each other better and she knew she could trust me.

"Why did you start an MC?" Alana asked suddenly as we pulled into the parking lot of her condo.

"That's a longish story. You maybe want to go for a walk and I'll tell you all about it?" I replied, putting the truck into park. She stared at me for a long time, her gaze roaming my face before she finally answered with "sure" and unbuckled her seatbelt.

"There's a park across the street," she said, coming to stand beside me. "You wanna go over there?"

"Sure." I said. I couldn't tell if she realized this wasn't going to be an easy conversation or if she was finally getting to be comfortable with me but when I took her hand to walk across the street she didn't pull away.

CHAPTER 6

Alana

A long ish story that was obviously not going to be easy to tell, yup totally picked up on that vibe. I should have pulled my hand out of his, but when he linked his fingers with mine I just couldn't.

His hands were so big and so warm I couldn't force myself to pull away. We walked for quite a while through the park before he squeezed my fingers and started to speak.

"I was in the CAF." He said quietly.

"CAF, Canadian Armed Forces?"

"Yeah."

"War." I stated, understanding now why this conversation would be difficult.

"Yeah," He exhaled. "Special Forces, remember Axle?"

"How could I forget?" I snorted, remembering that day over a week ago I had met Lo's VP.

"We served together. Did basic training and all that together and were stationed together just outside Ottawa then sent first to Iraq and then Afghanistan. We each did three six year contracts before retiring. We were lucky, we were at the end of our contracts and able to choose not to re-up but while we came out of the Sand Box physically in one piece, mentally and emotionally we were broken.

"We did a few years of therapy trying to get to a point where we could function in society. We rented a two room apartment so we could keep an eye on each other and found through all the shit we did, taking courses so we could open a business and put our other skills to use. We really missed the lifestyle." He smirked at that, like he couldn't believe he called the military a lifestyle.

"What do you mean? What did you miss, war?"

"Yes." He said simply, "But at the same time no. It was more the brotherhood, knowing that the guy beside you had your back and would die for you. Both Axle and I knew we still had each other but it's different having twenty or so guys, like a giant extended family."

"I guess you form some pretty serious and tight bonds in situations like that."

"You have an amazing way of understating things." He laughed. "But you're right. Axle and I had been friends before we joined and we went through some heavy shit in the eighteen years we were in together. When we got back we tried to stay in Ontario but oddly enough the area held some pretty horrible memories. Even moving to different parts of the province didn't help so we decided to move as far from home as possible. When we got back we were missing the adrenalin rush of war and found the safest way to get that back was riding motorcycles."

"How long have you been in Kamloops?" I asked, squeezing his hand, letting him know I was listening and what he was telling me was important to me.

"About five years. Axle and I sat down one night after he had a hard session with the therapist and I was pissed off at my boss and work and just feeling wrung out, done. We decided that night over beer that we would move as far as we could and we would gather together other guys like us. There had to be a lot of them, right?

"So here we are, the War Angels MC. Our name didn't come about because we're angels of war or we liked war, but for all the men and women we lost to war. Hopefully in the last five years we've given the forty or so guys we've got with us somewhere safe to decompress and come back and still be useful."

"You talk about the men and women you fought with and lost over there but you don't have any women in your club."

"Not for any reason." He shrugged. "Just haven't had any women stumble through our doors looking to join. Probably the stereotype of MCs is an all-male thing, but we're not completely closed to the idea of having women with us as members and not just in our beds."

We were silent for a while as we walked, me thinking about all the things he had told me and him, I'm sure getting his emotions back under control.

"Where did you learn sign language?" I was really curious about that.

"You remember Hammer? The guy at the door the other day, you told him you would shove his dick so far up his ass he would taste his own jizz." Understanding must have shown on my face because Lo chuckled and continued. "His last tour his convoy was hit by an IED and his voice box was crushed. Took a lot of rehab but the doctors he hadn't been sure he'd ever talk again. It was easier at the time to learn sign than always have pen and paper available. Especially since most of us have chicken scratch and atrocious spelling."

"How are you now? You've been out for how many years?"

"Seven years."

"So, you and Axle and Hammer, are you living or surviving?" I asked as I stopped walking and pulled him to look at me. He stared at me quietly for a minute searching my face for something.

He must have found whatever it was because he dipped his head and rested his forehead on mine. He closed his eyes and his thick lashes rested on his cheeks as he took a few deep breaths. Then he nudged my nose with his and touched his lips softly to mine. We both gasped a deep breath but took the kiss no further.

"I thought we were living, or at least I was." He whispered when he broke away. "But now I think I was just surviving, waiting for you." That kind of took me by surprise. The big bad ass biker had a sensitive side, he was kind of poetic.

"Oh yeah?" I replied, "You think you were waiting for my insanity, my six kids and my busy life chasing after them? Well, welcome to the zoo, these are my monkeys."

"Yeah, I was definitely waiting for you and your monkeys. Shit flinging and all."

"Hey! I trained that out of them years ago! Now they just fling cleverly worded insults." I smirked up at this man who was quickly burrowing his way into my heart.

Lo threw his head back and laughed as though it had been building up and was locked deep inside and he could finally let it go. Emotional release came in many different ways, thankfully for Lo it came in the form of laughter.

CHAPTER 7

Lo

"Hey Prez," I looked up to see Axle walking across the shop towards me. It had been almost a week since my lunch with Alana. We hadn't seen each other again but we had texted or talked on the phone, or both every day. I had just been thinking to myself how things had changed after only a week.

Alana had blown into our clubhouse hell bent on hating us and I was at the point of giving no fucks about her or her shit. Now, we were something else. I couldn't keep my mind off of her and I missed her all the time.

I had believed that I would be alone with a few casual relationships here and there, but I had never met a woman I really wanted to get to know, or that I wanted to keep around for more than a few weeks. Alana had turned my world on its head.

"What's up, Axle?"

"You might wanna come and see what Seether has found in Demon's shit." Seether had been looking through all of Demon's papers and stuff that we didn't donate after he died.

As soon as he opened one file it led him to another and another and another and two days ago we found ourselves standing outside a fully packed storage unit. Not only did Demon have more papers legal and otherwise, but he also had more bikes, a car and he had actually set up an office in the storage unit.

"Fuck, I doubt I want to, but I'm sure I should. Demon is coming back from the grave to bite us in the ass, brother." I put my wrench down as I slid out from under a Dodge Charger I was changing the oil on.

"Ain't that the truth, Prez?" I followed Axle back into the club house to the store room we were using to house all Demons' shit.

His room had already been given to another prospect so we had to move all the alcohol for the bar into the kitchen to have the space for it all. As we walked past the bar Axle grabbed three beers. I looked at my watch then back at my brother, it was only ten in the morning.

"Seriously, you're gonna need it. And Seether asked for one."

I heaved a sigh as I stood outside the door of the room where Seether was sitting on the floor surrounded but piles and stacks of paperwork and files.

"Fuck, boss." He said when he noticed us. "Where's my fuckin' beer?"

"What's going on, Seether." I asked seemingly calm but knowing if Seether was this worked up about something that something was really bad. I waited for Axle to pass Seether the bottle of beer he had brought and we all took a pull, waiting for Seether to calm.

"Demon was a narc."

"The fuck you say?" That got my attention. "Who was he narking on? We aren't involved in that shit."

"Yeah well, according to Demon's files there was or is a Fed that thinks we are and is hell bent on taking us down. Some guy out of Quebec, dealt a lot with the Hells Angels out there and has now warped his brain into believing that all MCs are corrupt 1%ers."

"What's this guys' name?" Axle asked, his beer now hanging loosely from his fingertips at his side. My friend was no longer relaxed and waiting patiently.

"Doesn't say an actual name just a code name, lots of code here, I'm guessing it's something he picked up overseas, but he was in and out of the forces before any of us so who knows what it all means. Looks, though like Demon thought this Fed was crooked himself and there's a lot of info here that could bury this guy. Did you all know Demon could draw?" Seether asked, holding up a perfect very detailed sketch of a man.

"What? Shit, not a chance. I've known Demon for over five years, that guy didn't have a single artistic bone in his body. Give me a minute to check something out." I said, pulling out my phone. Alana was an artist but she never mentioned doing portraits, I had to ask her though.

Babe, you ever draw faces?

Nope not my shtick, Chelle though does amazing portraiture.

Thanks babe. Coffee tonight, got some info for you.

Sure, wanna meet at that same place?

I know she meant the Tim Horton's we first had coffee at but that wasn't gonna cut it this time.

Nah babe, we're gonna need something stronger than French Vanilla. Can you come to the club house, as soon as you can get away?

Sure, all the boys have something going on tonight, I can ask my parents to pick them up and feed them. I'll come over around four?

Sounds good, see you then.

"Alana says Michelle, Demon's daughter, does portraits. How

much you wanna bet she drew that picture? Alana's coming over after school today and we'll get closer to the bottom of this then. Good work Seether, take a break, go play with your computers for a bit then get back to it, yeah?"

"Yeah Prez, this is a huge shit show, I need some tech time. A break from this old school paper shit Demon was buried in."

"Well," Axle sighed, "Whatever Demon was buried under in life it got him buried six feet under. I'm gonna go clean some stalls, gotta work off this energy."

If Axle was volunteering to muck horse stalls I knew he was upset. I clapped him on the shoulder and followed him out. I still had that Charger to finish and far too many other jobs in the shop to be taking much time off.

***

"Prez," I looked up to see Hammer standing at the front door to the clubhouse with Alana beside him. This time she was looking up at him with a genuine smile instead of the angry smirk she had the last time she was here.

"Hey babe, come on in." I stood up from the table I was at with Axle and met her half way across the room. "I gotta ask you a few questions about Michelle."

"Oh, is there something wrong with the legal papers for guardianship?" She asked, worrying her bottom lip with her teeth.

"No babe." I sighed, reaching up and gently pulling her lip free with my thumb. "I haven't been able to talk to our lawyer about that yet. Sharpie is a member and he knows basically what's going on but I've asked him to hold off on that stuff until we know more about what Demon was into."

"Oh." Her eyes dropped from mine, obviously disappointed.

"I'm not trying to trick you or run you around here babe. Just gotta protect the club."

"Ok." She nodded looking up at me again but her smile was not as bright. "So what did you need to talk to me about?"

"C'mon." I said taking her hand and pulling her behind me to the store room where Seether had all of Demon's shit spread out.

"Oh my," She sighed when she saw the mess. "What's this?"

"Alana, this is Seether, our tech guy."

"And all around genius," Seether smiled, rising from the floor to shake Alana's hand.

"See," Lo said, "Fat head."

Seether was a tall skinny fucker. I was big, but Seether was taller than me by at least three inches. He probably weighed about the same as I did but where I was full of muscle and worked out Seether was long and lanky.

He had muscle of his own, had to being in the CAF and he did work out but he had long lean muscle that made him look like a long distance runner. And run he did. It was his chosen method of staying in shape.

"Nice to meet you, ma'am."

"Oh sweetheart, please don't tell me I look old enough to be a ma'am." She smiled up at him, taking his hand in hers.

"No ma- I mean miss, just a habit from the forces." Seether blushed and squeezed her hand before putting both of his sheepishly in his pockets.

"Don't worry Seether, I understand. Compared to you I'm sure I am old enough to be a ma'am." She chuckled, obviously trying to put the nerd in front of her at ease. "So, what did you want to show me?"

"Babe, you ever seen this guy before?" I asked her, holding out my hand to take the drawing of the Fed from Seether to show her.

"Not in person." She shrugged. "Chelle has a few drawings of him in a sketchbook but nothing this detailed or precise. Who is he? Not Demon?"

"No babe, not Demon. Thanks Seether. Let's go to my room and we'll talk." I said putting slight pressure on her back to steer her out of the store room.

We walked quickly out of the kitchen and down the hall to the member's private rooms. Just as we passed Axle's room his door opened. He had a tee half way on and his hair was still wet from a shower.

"Glad to see you finally showered, you stank after working in the stalls."

"Thanks man, I'll take a bonus on my next check for that voluntary shit hauling." He smirked as we hurried past. At the last door we stopped and I pulled my keys from my pocket and unlocked my door.

There wasn't a lot in my room, a king sized bed and nightstand, tall dresser with a big screen TV on top, a large microfiber rocker recliner, a set of shelves with a stereo system, books and dvds, closet and full size bathroom. The curtains on the window were open letting light from the late afternoon in.

"Nice," Alana said, stepping through the door and scanning the space. "Utilitarian and clean."

"Army chic," I smirked at her.

"But not green."

"Nope, had enough green and brown overseas, much prefer blue."

I replied looking around at the pale blue walls and dark blue bedding. The furniture itself was a sturdy wood. "I would actually prefer everything to be white but white is not a colour conducive to my job."

"Yeah, as a mother, I can see being very angry if one of my boys brought me white bedding to wash with horse shit or grease stains all over it." I chuckled with her then became serious.

"I missed you this week." I whispered, lifting my hand to tuck a strand of her hair behind her ear then cupping her jaw.

"We talked every day." She whispered back, lifting her face to mine just slightly.

"Not the same." I grunted then pulled her to me and slammed my lips to hers. I licked the seam of her lips silently asking permission for entrance into her mouth. She complied readily with a whimper and sucked in a breath.

She was warm and tasted like coffee and mint and heaven. Her hands came up to my shirt and grabbed fistfuls before one snaked around my neck and buried in my hair.

My own hands were not still. The one on her jaw slid up to the back of her head into her soft hair and grasped the strands there, tugging slightly. The other dropped slowly to her hip and around to cup her ass. She whimpered again as I pulled away to catch my breath and started walking us back towards my bed.

Just before her knees came into contact with the edge of the mattress I kissed her lips again softly, my tongue licking inside then trailed my mouth down from her ear to her shoulder, pulling her leg up around my hips before I lifted her slightly and we toppled back onto the bed. I pulled my hand from her hair to brace us so I didn't crush her.

"Wait." She gasped as I sucked on the skin over her collar bone that was exposed by the open collar of her blouse. "Lo, please, wait." I nipped her skin once more before I pulled back to look into her eyes.

"What's wrong?" I asked, drowning in the desire I saw in her eyes. We were both breathing heavily like we'd just run a race but were both unsatisfied.

"We can't." She whispered, closing her eyes, getting herself under control.

"Why not, you're not married or underage are you?" I asked, licking up her neck to her chin and nipping her again with my teeth.

"No, neither, but you and I aren't married and while I don't exactly expect you to wait until we are, we barely know each other. I may not be perfect but I do believe in the sanctity of marriage and I feel jumping into bed with you so quickly is setting a really poor example for my boys." Her soft fingers were brushing through the hair that was falling over my forehead. She was nervous; I could see it in her eyes and feel it in the trembling of her hands. "I want to, Lo but I'm not ready. We're not ready."

CHAPTER 8

Alana

"Okay babe." Lo sighed, pushing himself off of me but not completely away. His hand left my hip to adjust his pants.

"I'm sorry." I said, watching his face for a reaction.

"Don't be sweetheart, I understand, I really do." He said pressing a soft kiss to my lips.

"You're not mad?"

"I'm not happy, and neither is my dick, but no, I'm not mad." He brushed my hair away from my face and placed his palm at the base of my throat. My breath caught and I moaned at the heat and weight of his hand resting against me.

"Babe," he groaned, tucking his face into my neck. "You can't make noises like that if you're not going to let me in you."

"Sorry." I whispered. "Um, I know this is a lot to ask, um especially now, but could you hold me? You can say no, I'll understand completely. As a matter of fact, forget I said anything." I tried to scramble off the bed and away from him but he grabbed and pulled me back to him.

"Come here. I'll always hold you." He said pulling us up to the head of the bed and wrapping his arms around me, pulling me to sprawl across his chest and kissing the top of my head.

"I'm too heavy to lay on you like this." I said trying to pull back slightly.

"Don't be ridiculous." He scoffed. "I weigh well over two hundred pounds, if your hundred and eighty was too heavy I'd be a fucking pussy. Stay here where you belong."

We stayed that way for a few minutes, me breathing his scent deeply into my lungs, my hand resting on his chest then moving slowly up to his jaw and running my fingertips over the stubble there. His hand behind me ran up and down my back from my neck to the waistband of my jeans, soothing me like a skittish kitten and his other hand gripped my hip, holding me close to him.

"So, what did you want to tell me about Demon?" I asked quietly. Heaving a deep sigh Lo reached to the side and grabbed a remote off the nightstand. Seconds after pointing it behind me Metallica started to play quietly.

"You know the Canadian government has a federal branch, the RCMP right? There's a branch called D Division. It's the area that deals with drug enforcement."

"Ok, I remember Demon was caught in a drug raid but how is that linked to the federal government?"

"Because there's a federal agent that seems to think the club is dirty. We're not, never have been but this guy has it in his head that all MCs are like the Hells Angels. He's looking to eradicate us all. I don't know what he had on Demon to get him to cooperate but there was nothing for him to find here. Seether's still looking through all Demons' shit, but that's what we've found so far." Lo's arm tightened around my shoulders and pulled me farther across his chest.

"That drawing you showed me . . . ?"

"Yeah, we think that's the Fed."

"That's Chelle's work. She drew that. Do you think Demon had her do it? Like a police sketch of sorts?" I asked, lifting up to look in his eyes.

"Either that or he showed up at their house or she got a look at him and felt something was off. You think you can ask her about it?"

"Yeah, of course, I'll ask her tonight." I replied, dropping my head back to Lo's chest then pushing my nose under his jaw and taking a deep breath.

"Did you just sniff me?" He demanded his chest bouncing as he chuckled.

"Shut up, you smell really good." I mumbled, feeling my face heat, positive my cheeks were a bright red.

"Babe, I gotta ask you about before."

"Before what Lo?"

"Before when we were kissing, have you been with anyone since your husband?"

"No."

"At all?"

"No Lo, believe it or not there hasn't been much opportunity to date or become attached to someone enough to actually want to have sex with them. You would be the first since my husband died." I sighed tucking my head down and running my fingers over the ridges of muscle pushing through his shirt.

"It's not a bad thing babe." His hand settled over mine, stopping my movements. "What do your boys think of you dating?"

"I haven't talked to them about it. I didn't know I was dating anyone." I said cheekily lifting up and piling my hands on his chest, resting my chin on them to look at him.

"I think after today babe you can safely say you're dating some-one."

"Oh yeah, who's that? I'd love to tell my boys his name."

"Smart ass," He laughed and smacked my ass just as his stomach growled. "I guess I'm hungry, you wanna get something to eat with me?"

"Sure, but do we have to go out? We could go back to my place and I could cook something. All of my kids will be there but it will give me a chance to talk to Chelle about that drawing. And you'd get a chance to meet her."

"Nah, we can stay here. The kitchen's stocked, I'll make dinner. I want to know about what Demon was into before I meet Mi-chelle. I want to have more information for her. Her dad was a good guy but I don't think given their history that she knows that."

"You're probably right." I agreed. "Before moving here from the Island she didn't even know he existed. She knew he was alive somewhere, but that was it. Her mom never talked about him. She said he was nice to her but obviously didn't know what to do with a teenage girl let alone a kid."

"Why do you call her Chelle?"

"Hmm, Drew. With his deafness he can't always say all the letter sounds and if he's excited then he skips them all together in his hurry to get his words out. When he met her he was so excited to bug Nate about his girlfriend he kept calling her Mm-chelle. We all thought it was cute and when Chelle heard it she got the big-gest sweetest smile on her face. It was obvious she loved it so it stuck."

"Sounds like you got some pretty awesome kids babe."

"Yeah," I said smiling wistfully. "I do. You got any kids tucked away anywhere Lo?"

"Nope, never met anyone I wanted more than to spend a little time with. Besides, my life with the CAF wasn't exactly conducive to family life." He smirked.

"Do you want kids of your own now, Lo?"

"Why you acting so pensive babe? You worried about my answer?"

"Yeah, a little." I replied. "After Drew was born I had to have an emergency hysterectomy Lo. If you want kids of your own I can't give them to you."

"Babe, I never in my life wanted a woman enough to want to have kids with her. Would I love for you to get big and round with my kid and to share that with you? Fuck, hell yeah I would, but it's not a deal breaker. If it were possible for you to one day far in the future to give me our kid that would be amazing, but there are far more factors then just you not having the plumbing."

"Lo!" I snorted on a laugh.

"Seriously babe, I'm forty-three, I only just got you and I'm feeling like sharing you with the kids you've already got is gonna be hard, but ... " he held up a finger before I could interrupt him. "They got you first and I understand and accept they need you more than I do. I'm 100% ok with that. Even if you were physically able to have more kids you already said you're over forty –"

"Forty-one."

"There, forty-one. By the time our relationship was ready for kids our bodies wouldn't be able to handle it."

"Lo, what did I do to deserve you?"

"Nothing babe, that implies that you had to achieve or win me. You don't, you just get me. And I just get you and we get to keep each other because we work hard for it. Now come on, let's get you fed and home to your brood." He kissed me once more and pushed me to my feet and followed me.

***

"Chelle, can I talk to you?" I said later that night after the younger boys went to bed. Chelle and Nate were sitting at the kitchen table doing homework together, talking about the lab they had done in science that morning.

"Of course Mrs. M." Chelle said looking up at me and smiling. She was such a sweet girl I hated to see the pain and sadness lurking behind her eyes.

"I noticed a couple of drawings of a man in your sketchbook. Can you tell me who he is?"

"I don't know." Chelle shrugged. "He came to the house once months before my dad disappeared and I saw him talking to my dad. My dad had just come home from somewhere and was in the driveway when that guy showed up. It was like first thing in the morning and I was on my way to school and was just leaving the house. I walked up to my dad to say hi and bye and he told me to get back into the house. I was kinda shocked 'cause dad usually just grunted and nodded at me when other people were around. I looked right at that guy then turned and went back into the house. It was like the second or third week of school."

"Did that man talk to you? Or do you remember what he and your dad were talking about? Did your dad tell you anything about him?"

"No, the guy just looked at me with a strange smile on his face. Dad said if I ever saw him around I should go straight to the clubhouse, that's why I was surprised when you said the guys there didn't know who I was. I figured dad wouldn't have told me to go there if they didn't know who I was. After that guy left dad came in and asked me to draw him. Took a couple of tries but I guess I got it good enough that he was satisfied."

"What's this about, Mom?" Nate asked sitting back in his chair and crossing his arms over his chest. He had been listening quietly until this point but was no longer happy to stay quiet. "I remember that day. You never miss school Chelle, I figured you were sick but you were back at school the next day and looked fine. We weren't friends yet so I couldn't ask you about it."

"That guy your dad had you draw is a federal agent with D Division. That's the Canadian version of the DEA." I said, sighing. "Lo thinks that guy had something on your dad to make him work for him trying to bring the War Angel MC down. Lo can't figure it out, though because the MC has never been involved in that and their members aren't allowed to use drugs."

"Dad didn't even smoke." Chelle said, shrugging. "That was one thing my mom told me about him. She said she loved him so much but he was broken."

"Chelle, how much do you know about the MC your dad was a part of?"

"Nothing Mrs. M, dad didn't tell me anything." Chelle shrugged again.

"Lo and his VP Axle started the MC when they both left the CAF and needed the structure of a brotherhood. All the members of the club are veterans who have been through a lot since leaving the CAF and needed help reintegrating into society. They all want to meet you, sweetie. They all have so much respect for your dad and they're all just as confused as you are by all this."

"Really Mrs. M, they're probably more confused by it all. They all knew him a lot better than I did." Chelle sighed then went back to her homework. I watched her for a second then looked up to see Nate watching me. I nodded to him to follow me out of the room.

"Keep an eye on her, Nate." I said quietly when we were out of ear shot.

"You know I will mom." I smiled and hugged my son. I jumped back a second later and really looked at him. "When the hell did you get so tall?"

"Um, last year?"

"Not funny, I swear last year you weren't as tall as me."

"Wrong mom, I've been at least as tall as you for a while now." Nate chuckled and went back to the kitchen to finish his homework.

The rest of the week progressed like normal. Or as normal as you can get running around like a crazy person after a village of children after working mostly full time, meeting people to work on their tatts and sitting down to write something, anything. Thanks to Lo and his club I certainly didn't have a shortage of inspiration.

I even found time after school in the middle of the week to have coffee with a friend. Brooke was the kindergarten teacher at our school and she was one of the greatest people I knew. She always seemed so cheerful and I had always wanted to get to know her better but our work schedules and my kids made that close to impossible. Now I was determined to change that.

"Seriously Brooke, you're single?" I demanded as she sipped her tea.

"Sure, so what?" She shrugged and smiled at me.

"But you're so young; don't you want to get married?"

"I haven't really thought about it for a while. Since I discovered my calling wasn't a convent I've just sort of left it all in God's hands."

"Wow, I think you're much stronger than I am. When I was younger I considered a convent for about five seconds."

"Nah, I'm not stronger than you, just a different kind of strong. You have to be strong for other reasons." Her lips tipped up a little on one side and she sipped her tea again. I watched this young woman in front of me for a moment, taking in her inner beauty as well as the more obvious outer beauty.

Her long platinum blonde hair was pulled back in a low ponytail and cascaded down her back to her waist. When she looked up at me her perfect complexion glowed and her soft blue eyes sparkled. Her smile widened to show perfect white teeth when she looked up and found me staring.

"What?"

"Nothing," I said, "You're just spectacular." She snorted then stood and excused herself to use the washroom.

"Alana!" I turned to find Axle and Hammer at the door to the café. Both men strode toward me and I waited, watching these giant men swagger across the store. "You here alone, doll?"

"No Axle, I'm here with a friend from work. What are you guys doing here? You don't seem like the specialty coffee types." Hammer smirked and looked around the store.

"Nah, we're not. We were across the street at the A&W getting a late lunch and Hammer saw you through the window. He said you were sitting here with an angel."

"Ha! You have no idea." I laughed, shaking my head. "Oh, here she comes, I'll introduce you guys." Brooke came back to the table and smiled quietly at the two men as she sat down. "Brooke, these are Logan's friends Axle and Hammer. Guys, this is Brooke, she teaches kindergarten at our school."

"It's nice to meet you." Brooke said politely, smiling but offered nothing more. The guys nodded and grunted, saying hello then turned back to me but I noticed Axle's gaze kept returning to Brooke once in a while.

"Did Lo tell you about the party at the club house Saturday?" Axle asked.

"No, he never mentioned it." I replied, shrugging my shoulders. It was only Wednesday, not like he didn't have a lot of time to bring it up if he wanted to.

"It's a kind of good bye for Demon. I'm sure Lo will tell you next time he talks to you. You should bring your friend with you."

"We'll see." I replied, not wanting to put Brooke on the spot. I was sure even if she did drink she wasn't up for a biker party. The guys chatted for a few more minutes then did that chin jerk they did and left.

"Axle, Hammer and Demon huh?" Brooke laughed.

"Yeah," I replied, "I'm not sure where the names come from but I can't imagine a mother purposefully naming her child Demon, or Hammer. Could you imagine? What would that conversation even sound like? The doctor puts the baby on your chest and you look at your husband and say 'Oh look dear, our darling little boy looks like he was smashed in the face with a hammer! I know! That's what we should call him! Hammer!'"

"Oh but then your loving husband says 'No sweetheart, look at his misshapen head! We should definitely call him Demon!'" Brooke and I laughed so hard we almost spilled our drinks. It was at that moment that my phone chimed with a text message.

"Sorry," I chuckled, "Better check it in case it's the boys." I pulled my phone out and found a text from Lo.

Hey babe, I just got a text from Axle reminding me not so nicely that I hadn't invited you to the party Saturday. He also not so nicely told me I should tell you to bring the angel. WTF??

"Haha!" I laughed, looking up at Brooke. "We were just officially invited to the party this weekend. Do you want to go?"

"Umm, I don't know. What exactly does a biker party entail?" She asked, biting her lip apprehensively.

"Couldn't tell you, let me ask."

What would be expected of the angel and I at this party?

I shot back. I could definitely understand Brooke's trepidation.

Show up, have fun. Drink if you wanna, don't if you don't. A couple of girls will be there but mostly wives and girlfriends.

You mean ol' ladies?

What? Babe my beer just came out my nose.

Sorry, just getting the lay of the land as such. The angel, AKA Brooke, is really . . . shall we say . . . innocent? Is this gonna freak her out and send her screaming for the hills?

Nah, there'll be booze yeah, but we're all pretty tame. Like I said before, no drugs and any girls who will be there want to be there. Given that this is sort of a memorial for Demon we'll make sure everyone keeps their clothes on and takes their rendezvous to their bedrooms.

Ok, I'll tell her. I'll be there for sure, can't guarantee the angel, though.

Ok babe. I'll call you later.

"Ok, so no drunken orgies, at least not in the common rooms and any hookers are there of their own accord. Lo promises to make them all keep their clothes on." Brooke snorted at me and rolled her eyes. "Lo says the party is more of a memorial for a guy that died not that long ago. You know Michelle at school, in Nate's class? It's her dad that died."

"I thought the news said her dad died as part of a drug raid or something."

"He did, but that behaviour is not typical of the club. There are no drugs with these guys. Demon was into other shit."

"Ok, I'll think about going for a little bit. But how about I meet you there in case I need to leave early?"

"Sounds good to me," I replied smiling. We chatted for a bit longer then said our goodbyes and went our separate ways promising to see each other at school the next day.

CHAPTER 9

Lo

"What was with the beer hose out the nose?" Seether asked me when I put my phone back in my pocket after texting with Alana.

"I was asking Alana about coming to the party on the weekend and she asked for details. I told her some wives and girlfriends would be here and she asked if they were like ol' ladies."

"Holy fuck!" Seether laughed. "She read a lot of romance novels or what?"

"Nope, she writes 'em."

"Shit. You're in trouble brother."

"Ain't that the truth?" I said taking another pull on my beer as I watched the men scattered around the room. Seether had found out a lot from Demon's papers and files but there was still something missing.

His house had been sold and since we didn't know about it all the stuff that was in it had been taken to the landfill and was now lost to us. If there had been anything of importance in there it was gone. We had passed everything we had on to Sharpie to deal with the legalities but something about it all was still bugging me.

"What's the matter? You're scowling like you stepped in dog shit."

"You're a fucking poet you know that Seether?"

"Nah just calls 'em as I sees 'em."

"We're missing something about this shit with Demon." I replied shrugging

"Sure as shit we are brother. Been bugging the hell outta me the last couple of days since we turned it all over to Sharpie, don't know what to do about it though." Seether heaved a sigh and tipped his head back to look at the ceiling. "I was hoping if I left it for a while something would come to me but there ain't nothin' comin'."

"That what you tell all the girls?" Axle asked as he sat at the table with us, Hammer right behind him.

"Hardly," Seether snorted, "More like 'Get ready bitches! Here it comes!'"

"There is no fuckin' way! Not with a pencil dick like a skinny fuck like you has to have!" Axle roared with laughter.

"Hey, I have no problems pullin' it out and measuring right here and now fucker." Seether chuckled, holding his hands up. I've known all these men for years, without actually looking you tend to see a lot you don't want to see. Not all of our parties have been as tame as the one on Saturday is going to be. Drunken threesomes and hook ups in the main room of the clubhouse are not always out of the questions. Sober ones either.

This same conversation has been had after a lot less alcohol and the threats to show proof have been followed through on. Seether might be a tall skinny fucker but the dude was hung like a fucking horse. And Axle, only a couple of inches shorter than I was, also never left the ladies he was with complaining.

Hammer and I just shook our heads and chuckled at the antics of our brothers.

"Not that kind of a party this time, boys." I said taking a swallow from my beer.

"Nope, Axle's angel is coming this time." Hammer rasped snickering.

"Fuck you, she's not my angel, she just looks like a fucking angel. Seether, pull out your phone or tablet or whatever the hell you've got on you and look up the school Alana works at." Axle demanded waving his hand at Seether, their dick measuring contest forgotten.

Seether did as directed and handed the tablet sized phone across the table. Axle searched through the site for a few minutes then finally pushed the tablet over to me.

"There, see? She's fucking ethereal or some shit."

Seether and I looked down at the photo of the woman on the screen. Axel was right, as hard as it was to tell from a picture she had to be tiny. Her white blonde hair was pulled back in a ponytail that hung over her shoulder and her smiling, soft blue eyes shone. Seether whistled low and shook his head.

"A fucking kindergarten teacher man?" Seether asked, "You sure that's a good idea? You're gonna spend one night at her place and come back here after craft night with your dick all covered in glitter and shit and you'll have to build a set of shelves for your new finger puppet collection."

"You're a fuckin' dick." Axle laughed at Seether, flicking the cap from his beer bottle across the table hitting Seether in the center of the forehead.

"Hey Prez, you got a minute?" Sharpie had walked up to us while we were laughing at Seether and Axle's antics. He was not laughing with us. I immediately sobered and stood with our lawyer.

"Yeah man, let's go to the office. Ax-" I said leading my VP and

Sharpie out of the common room.

"Actually Prez, Hammer and Seether should come, too." Sharpie said following behind me. I nodded and whistled to the other guys to follow. When we were all seated around the desk in my office I nodded at Sharpie to begin. "Well, that raid that Demon was caught up in? The dealer the cops were actually after is out of prison. I got a hold of the agent who put Demon there but he wouldn't tell me what he had on Demon to get him to cooperate. He did say he knew we were clean and he wasn't looking into us."

"That's fucking bullshit." Axle exploded.

"I know Ax but I can't force him to tell me shit. I can only ask pointed questions and this dude is smart. He barely broke a sweat. He did apologize for how shit went down with Demon dying and all but he said more or less, them's the breaks." Sharpie shrugged, looking frustrated.

"Fucker," Hammer rasped tapping his fingers on his knee like he was having a hard time sitting still.

"Yup. So, he said that the reason he had tapped Demon was because he needed to take this dealer down ASAP and he didn't have time to set up a UC. True, false? I don't know, I don't think it matters at this point. He said he used Demon and gave him the cover that Demon was a liaison of sorts for the club because we wanted to get into the drug business."

"That's such fucking shit." Seether said, shaking his head. "Prez, most of us don't even smoke let alone get into any illegal shit. What the hell does this guy think we'd want to get into fuckin' drugs for?"

I was fucking tired of this shit. I sat forward in my chair and rested my elbows on my desk rubbing my face. Demon, the dumb fuck, had screwed us all. There had to be something we were missing.

"All right, for now Sharpie, cooperate with this Fed, but don't give him too much. At least we know Demon wasn't completely off the deep end. Seether is there absolutely nothing left in Demon's shit that can answer some of these questions?"

"No Prez, I've been through Demon's shit three times forward and backward. The only thing I haven't figured out is the shit he's got in code. It's not a lot, just a couple of pages but I've typed it into every search engine in the universe. I've tried every cipher known to man and I still can't break it."

It wasn't often Seether got angry but right this moment he was seething.

"All right then, that's where we'll concentrate our efforts," I sighed, scratching the back of my neck. "Any time anyone has free time they need to be working on this code, whatever it is."

"I got an idea." Hammer said, trying to clear his throat.

"Sign it brother, don't force it." I said watching my brother struggle. He must be pretty stressed out if his throat was bothering him to the point that he couldn't even whisper a sentence.

There's gotta be some vets in the area that are older than us. Like closer to Demon's age. Can't we look them up and see if they know the code? Or if they have any idea what the cipher might be?

"Fuck Hammer! That's fucking genius!" Seether jumped up and ran out of the room. I knew from experience we wouldn't see him for a few hours. I looked over at Hammer who just shrugged and walked out of the room.

"Thanks for your hard work Sharpie," I sighed, shaking the man's hand. "As much as I hate you having to meet with that douche nozzle I'm still glad it was you and not me. You think this dealer is after the club now that he's out of prison?"

"According to the Fed he is." Sharpie nodded then promised to be back Saturday for the party.

"Douche nozzle?" Axle snickered at me.

"Something Alana said," I chuckled. "I called her the other night and she picked up the phone just as Cal screamed at Jack that he was a douche canoe for something or other and she screamed at both of them that calling anyone any kind of douche anything was not appropriate then under her breath she called them all douche nozzles. Fuckin' hilarious kids' man."

"You know what we haven't done in a long time?" I looked at Axle, waiting for him to continue. "Family bar-b-que. It's warm enough to have another one. I bet Alana's kids would love it. You planning on keeping her?"

"Fuck man, yeah I'm keeping her, for as long as she'll fucking have me."

"Then I bet a family bbq would go a long way to showing her you're safe with her kids."

"First Seether, then Hammer and now you, I'm surrounded by fucking geniuses! Weekend after this one, it'll be hot as hell and school should be out for the summer."

"Hey brother, I'm not the only genius in the room." Axle chuckled then walked out. Now that we had as much settled as we could with Demon's pile of shit I knew I had been neglecting the other brothers.

Especially Hammer. If his throat was bothering him so much that he would rather sign then talk I was totally missing something. Sighing heavily I heaved myself out of my chair and made my way down the hall to the private rooms and knocked on Hammer's door.

There was a thump from the other side which I guessed was a shoe or something hitting the door signaling that it was safe to enter. I opened the door a bit and looked in before I went in all the way.

"Hammer, you doin' alright?" He was on his bed facing the wall and rolled over onto his back when I closed the door.

My throat fucking hurts man. Hammer signed wearily.

"Worse than usual man?"

Way worse. Not sure what's going on but I made an appointment with the doctor to get it checked. For all I know it's just a bit of an infection but it feels like fire.

"Fuck, you take any pain killers?"

You know I can't.

"No, Hammer. I know you won't. An Advil or something isn't going to send you back into addiction. You don't have to suffer like this."

No, I can't risk it. I won't risk it. I can't go back to that place.

"All right man, I get it. Let me know if I can do anything to help." Hammer nodded then rolled back over towards the wall. I turned and let myself out of his room and went to my own to call Alana.

CHAPTER 10

Alana

Saturday night had arrived, the night of Demon's party. I still didn't know if Brooke was going to the party but as much as I would have liked her to go it didn't really matter. Maybe the end of the year bbq Lo had mentioned would be more her pace.

I hadn't said anything to Lo, but I had decided I was definitely going to take him to bed tonight and hopefully there wouldn't be much sleeping. We had been seeing each other, or dating or whatever you want to call it for just over a month.

Normally I would make any guy wait much longer than that to get into my pants, but Lo wasn't just any guy. He was Lo, he was something special.

I dressed carefully for this party, choosing dark skinny jeans and a sequined tank top and no ballet flats for this girl tonight. I pulled my biker chic boots out of my closet and put them on. They didn't have a huge heel, but they did give me a little lift, and let's face it, my boyfriend was a biker, it only made sense.

My boys and Chelle were sleeping over at my mom and dad's so no one would know if I didn't come home tonight, gotta love Oma and Opa.

When I pulled into the clubhouse parking lot I noticed there were a lot of bikes and trucks already there and the music was loud enough that I could hear it through the closed windows of my SUV. The place was packed.

I jumped out of my car and walked, hopefully confidently, into the clubhouse. I looked for Lo at his usual table but I didn't see him there. I looked for Axle or Hammer or even Seether but I didn't see any of them. I didn't know anyone else in the club yet so I was a little lost.

I had almost convinced myself to go down to Lo's room to see if he was there when warm, muscled arms wrapped around me and pulled me into a hard chest. I leaned back and took a deep breath of Lo. God he smelled amazing! I reached one arm up and behind me to grasp the back of his neck while I tilted my face up to look at his chin.

"You lookin' for me babe?" He rumbled behind me. I smiled as I turned in his arms and reached up on tiptoe to kiss his lips.

"I sure as hell was, but now that you found me I guess my search is over." I replied, sliding both my hands up into his hair. From the flare of his eyes I knew he got my double meaning. I was seriously falling for this guy, I could definitely love him. Lo growled low in his throat as his hands slid from my upper back down into the back pockets of my jeans.

"Fuck babe, you better be careful what you say. I just might think you mean more than you do." He said squeezing my ass.

"Think away Lo. Wouldn't say it if I didn't mean it."

"You're mine babe, in all ways, soon."

"I am yours Lo, in all ways, tonight."

"Fuck, you're killing me." He said as he sucked in a breath and nipped my jaw then trailed kisses around until he covered my mouth with his and licked inside.

The kiss was long and deep and full of promise and when he finally pulled away we were both breathing hard. I whimpered when he nipped my bottom lip then soothed it with his tongue. I licked the same spot to taste him just a little more and he moaned.

"Babe, I can't leave yet but you had better fuckin' believe as soon as I can I'm taking you to my room and locking the door until morning."

"Don't wait too long, Lo." I whispered in his ear, licking around the shell, "I don't know if I can wait very long for you." He moaned again as I pulled out of his arms and sauntered to the bar to get a drink.

CHAPTER 11

Lo

After Alana told me what she had planned for our night I almost couldn't keep my head straight. I introduced her to a few of the girlfriends and wives who were around and the members they were attached to and she spent most of the night on the dance floor shaking her ass. When she needed a drink she skipped over and plopped herself in my lap and wiggled her ass until I was so hard I hurt.

At the moment she was dancing again with her head thrown back and her arms up in the air. She looked absolutely amazing and I was just about ready to explode. I looked at my watch and saw it was past midnight.

Fucking perfect, if I disappeared now with my woman no one would really notice. Just as I was standing up an old Bryan Adam's song came on the juke. I pulled her into my arms as Adam's started singing about heaven and all he wants is the woman lying in his arms right now. It was perfect. She melted into me and attached her mouth to my neck and sucked hard.

Alana lifted her head just as I lowered mine and I took her mouth in a kiss that was hard and punishing. I needed her like I needed to breathe. We swayed to the music as we kissed until the tempo of the music changed and one of the brothers bumped my shoulder and told us to get a room.

Fuckin' A brother, I got the perfect fuckin' room.

I grabbed Alana's hand and pulled her behind me down the hall to my room. When we got there I turned her and pushed her back against the door and kissed her again. She eagerly met my lips with hers and licked inside my mouth, her hips arching against mine. I quickly, but clumsily dug in my jeans pocket for my keys to unlock the door.

"How drunk are you?" I demanded, tipping her head back with my thumb under her jaw so I could kiss and suck on her neck, shoving my keys into the lock and pushing the door open.

"I'm not. I had one beer and have been drinking diet coke the rest of the night. I wanted this too bad not to remember it in the morning." Her words made me growl and I pushed her back gently through the door.

I stepped inside and closed and locked the door, trying to get my breathing under control and losing the battle. I turned to her and tossed my keys on the book shelves and reached behind me to pull my shirt off.

I knew what I looked like, I wasn't stupid but when Alana gasped as I exposed my chest it was still very gratifying. I tossed my shirt on the chair and stepped to her, placing both my hands on her hips and ran them up her sides, pulling her top up with them and exposing her creaming skin.

When I first touched her she had been standing watching me with her hands at her sides but she quickly lifted them to grab my upper arms. Just before I pushed her arms over her head to take her shirt off her nails dug into my skin and squeezed leaving little half-moon indentations.

When her top was off she put her hands back on my arms and tipped her head back and pushed her breasts into my chest. For a split second before I lost my mind I looked down at her amazing tits and almost came in my pants.

"Alana," I groaned as I reached down and grabbed her ass in both hands and lifted, wrapping her legs around my waist. "I think I'm falling in love with you." I said as I kissed along her jaw then nipped her earlobe and sucked it into my mouth.

"You just think?" She gasped, rubbing her pussy against me through her jeans. "Me too, I need you Lo, now." I gave her one more kiss then tossed her on the bed and watched her bounce.

My hands fell to the button on my jeans and pulled the fly apart and shoved them down my legs, toeing off my boots and socks and leaving my jeans in a pile on the floor. Standing above her in only my boxer briefs that could barely hold my rock hard dick I let her look her fill.

CHAPTER 12

Alana

When I stopped bouncing on the bed I lay there and looked at Lo, my eyes caressing every inch of muscle and ink. Lo was built like a bodybuilder with muscles on his muscles, but surprisingly he didn't have a lot of tattoos like I would have assumed. His chest was heavily muscled and the ridges of his abs strained as he moved and stretched.

Just when I thought I was going to lose my mind from him not touching me he leaned over and pulled his wallet out of his pants and tossed a condom on the bed then lunged over me, kissing around my belly button and flicking his tongue into it.

"Lo," I moaned, arching my hips, wanting more. He kissed up my body until he got to my silk covered breasts and licked along the cups at the top of my bra, his big hands cupping my hips and holding me down on the bed.

He leaned over to the side to free one of his hands to reach up and pull my bra strap off my shoulder and the cup off my breast. Every inch of skin exposed by the bra he kissed until he came to my nipple and sucked it into his mouth.

"Lo, you're gonna kill me."

"You wet baby? You ready for me?" He demanded as he kissed across my chest to my other breast, rolling me slightly so he could undo the clasp at the back of my bra. "The fuck is this baby, chastity belt?" He grunted, struggling at my back.

"This is a bra that real women wear who have real breasts that are bigger than a C cup and have been used for their natural purpose." I chuckled darkly.

"Talkin' in riddles baby. Your taste has left me short a few brain cells." He said flipping me on my stomach and using both hands to undo the four eye hook clasp at my back.

"I have large breasts, Lo. I breastfed five boys, a little two hook clasp is not going to do much for these girls." I giggled.

"Baby, I fucking love your kids almost as much as I love you, but I don't really wanna talk about them while we're in bed together and I'm about to lick your pussy." Lo rasped, finally getting my bra undone and flipping me back, tossing my bra back over his shoulder.

He made quick work of the button on my jeans and pulled them off my legs, taking my panties with them. He stood staring down at me for a long minute until I started to squirm.

"Baby, you're fucking shaved." He moaned as he grabbed my ankles and spread my legs so he could push his shoulders between them, kissing up the inside of first one thigh and then the other.

"Lo, stop teasing." I gasped when he licked the crease at my hip.

"Oh baby, I'm just getting started." He said, running a finger from my entrance up to my clit and back down, pushing his finger inside me then pulling it out and adding another. "Fuck baby you're so wet and fucking tight. I make you this wet?"

"No Lo, it was that song before we came in here. Bryan Adams gets me every time." I moaned as he stroked in and out of me then whimpered when he stopped and pushed his thumb against my clit.

"Baby, you're lucky I know you're joking." He chuckled, starting to rub my clit in circles. "Don't talk about other men in our bed baby, even if they are rock stars you've never met." He pulled his fingers out of me and sucked them clean one at a time while watching me, his biceps jumping and flexing and his jaw clenching.

It was so hot I just about orgasmed right then and he wasn't even touching me. I threw my head back and arched my hips up, looking for his touch again but before I could ask for more he had buried his face between my legs and sucked my clit hard into his mouth, flicking it with his tongue.

"Lo, I need more, please, make me come!" I cried my head thrashing from side to side as his fingers entered me again and I came, my orgasm crashing over me harder than any orgasm I'd ever had.

When I started to come down again I could feel Lo's fingers stroking in and out of me, stretching me. When my legs finally stopped twitching he pulled back and shoved his briefs down his legs and grabbed the condom, lifting it to his lips to tear the packaged with his teeth.

"We don't need that." I said, wrapping one hand around his wrist and pulling his hand from his mouth and wrapping the other around his dick and stroking him from tip to root, rubbing the drop of pre-cum that seeped out along his length. And oh God the length and he was so thick. "I want to taste you first."

CHAPTER 13

Lo

"Fuck baby, if you put that wicked mouth on my cock right now I will explode in seconds. I wanna cum in your pussy the first time, not your mouth." I rasped, pulling her hand off my dick and pulling it above her head, trapping both her hands against the bed in one of mine, holding her there so I could put the condom on.

"Lo, we don't need a condom; I wanna feel you, not latex."

"Baby, you don't know what you're asking."

"Are you clean? I'm clean Lo, it's been six years since I had sex and even then it was with my husband. I get checked once a year and I can't get pregnant."

"I'm clean baby, I just got checked and it's been awhile since I was with anyone and even then I always gloved up."

"Please baby, I don't want anything between us." She moaned, grabbing handfuls of my hair and pulling me to her, kissing me like she was dying of thirst in the desert and I was the first drink of water she found. I wrapped my arm around her lower back and dragged her up the bed with me so her head was at least on a pillow.

"Be sure about this Alana." I said when she let me take a break from her lips. I looked deep into her eyes, finding a deep pool of golden desire. The dark chocolate and green flecks had disappeared to rim the outer edge and all that was left was gold. "If we do this now without a condom then we will never use one."

"Please Lo. Unless you're planning on having sex with someone else while you're with me then we don't need one." Without warning I surged into her and buried myself balls deep to the hilt until I couldn't sink any farther into her.

She cried out again and arched her hips up to meet mine, pushing her breasts into my chest. I waited a minute to let her get used to my size, knowing it had been years for her and I was far from small, no matter how wet she was she would need time to adjust.

"I'm not having sex with anyone but you for the rest of my life, Alana and you had better fucking believe this is more than just sex." I said when she started to squirm, pulling out of her, leaving only my tip inside her then surging again and attacking her mouth with mine, mimicking with my tongue what my dick was doing to her pussy. She was already tight and as her second orgasm started her inner walls clamped so tight around me I almost lost it right then and there.

"Lo!" She screamed as she came again, digging her nails into my shoulders so hard I was sure she would draw blood.

For sure I would be marked by her in the morning. I pistoned my hips in and out of her faster and faster until I felt my balls draw up and my cum shoot from me into her. I held myself tight against her until I was empty then collapsed onto her, holding myself just above on my arms so I didn't crush her.

She sighed as she came back to earth and I kissed her softly on the lips as she pulled her talons from my shoulders, trailing one hand into my hair and the other down my back, cupping my ass.

"Let me up babe and I'll clean you up." I said kissing her forehead.

"No Lo, I like you on me. Don't go yet." She whispered snuggling deep into my chest. I rolled to the side, pulling her with me and holding her close.

"You're fucking amazing, Alana."

"No Lo, your fucking is amazing." She giggled, tracing one of the tattoos on my chest. I snorted and swatted her ass. "Tell me about your tattoos, Lo."

"That one on my chest was my first. It's the insignia for JTF 2." I said as she traced the maple leaf and globe on either side of a sword.

"What's JTF 2?"

"Joint Task Force 2, it's a Special Operations Force branch of CAF."

"Special Operations are usually more secretive than regular branches of the military right?"

"Usually, regardless I can't tell you anything about where or when I served."

"That's ok." Alana shrugged, "I don't need to know those things. I might pick your brain for information when I'm writing a book, but otherwise the only time you have to tell me about any of it is if you want to. Or if you need to. I'm ok with that. What's this tattoo?"

"Those are angel wings and the numbers are service numbers for the men and women we lost overseas."

"It's beautiful Lo." She whispered, kissing the tattoo on my shoulder. "I had seen the numbers reaching from under your shirt sleeve and wondered what it was. This list is too long, Lo. It reaches from the top of your shoulder and ends at your elbow. That's too many good people dead."

"Ain't that the truth baby?" I said, holding her close to me. "Sleep now, I'm gonna need you again soon, you're gonna need your rest." She snorted but I felt her relax into me and soon her breathing slowed and I knew she was asleep.

The music from the main room was still loud so I knew the party was still going strong. I rubbed my face, wondering how the fuck I got to be so blessed. Alana sighed in her sleep as I hugged her close to me again and I felt myself slipping off into my own dreams of her.

It couldn't have been too much later when I was woken up by the bed shifting. I reached for Alana to pull her close to me again but my hands came back empty. I opened my eyes to find her sitting beside me cross-legged with her back to me.

"What are you doing, Alana?" I whispered my voice raspy from sleep.

"Oh! I'm sorry, did I wake you?" She asked, turning to me and I could see a sketchpad on her lap and a pencil in her hand with more tucked into her hair. When I looked past her I saw the bathroom light was on and the door was cracked open just enough to spill light onto her drawing.

"Only 'cause you weren't in my arms." I replied propping myself up on an elbow to see what she was working on. "What are you doing?"

"After talking about your tattoos, especially the last one I had an idea and it kept waking me up. I know from experience that if I don't draw it or write it down it will keep me up all night so I grabbed my sketchpad out of my purse." She was sitting on the bed wearing only my t-shirt from earlier talking a mile a minute.

"You left the room in only my t-shirt?" I demanded.

"No, well, I would have but when I opened the door Axle was just going into his room, I'm guessing with someone 'cause he closed the door really quick when he saw me. He was not happy about me leaving your room either and immediately demanded where I was going. I told him and he said to come back in here and he would go out to my truck for me. He's a nice guy." She said, her pencil never stopping on the page.

"What are you drawing babe?" She stopped drawing and tucked her pencil into her hair and turned to me, holding the sketchpad to her chest, hiding her work.

"Well see, after you told me about why you and Axle started the MC I really started thinking. I had seen Demon's vest –"

"It's called a cut babe."

"Right, so I had seen Demon's cut of course and noticed it was kind of boring. I mean, no offence, but a top and bottom rocker around wings, blah. And then you told me about the tattoo on your shoulder and I really got to thinking." She was talking fast again and looking around her. "Where's my damn pencil? We're going to get up in the morning with a bunch of pencils stuck in our asses, Lo. I keep losing them, I've lost like six!" Reaching up I pulled one of the five pencils from her hair and handed it to her. "Oh! Thanks."

Putting the pad back down to her lap she continued working. I let her work for a little bit and just watched her beautiful face. Every so often her forehead would crease and then her eyes would widen and sparkle and she would attack another part of the picture.

"So what was your thought that wouldn't let you sleep babe?" I yawned and looked at the clock beside the bed. It was 4 am which meant we had maybe gotten three hours of sleep.

"What? Oh, Lo I forgot you were there." She said distractedly. "So your patch is boring, just wings right, and the whole reason you started the MC was for soldiers who came back not quite whole. So I took the wings and spread them out like they were protecting the soldier kneeling in front of them like a shield.

"The soldier has his head bowed in prayer and he's holding dog tags. His weapon is standing beside him and he's holding it like it's a crutch keeping him upright. His helmet is lying upside down beside him with red and white poppies spilling out of it." She said as she drew and shaded. Finally she stopped and sighed then looked up at me.

"You gonna show me?" I asked, watching as she hugged the book to her chest again and closed her eyes then handed me the book. I took it from her but didn't take my eyes off her face but she kept her eyes closed, tipping her head back, letting her hair cascade down her back, the pencils tucked there falling to the floor forgotten.

"It's just a rough sketch, it still needs work." She whispered as she tipped her chin down and looked at me, her eyes the chocolate and gold colour but darker. Finally I took my gaze from hers and looked down at the drawing in my hand and froze.

CHAPTER 14

Alana

I wasn't sure what I was expecting. I didn't think Lo would hate it, but it was a drawing of something so personal to him and a memory so painful. I hadn't lied when I said I wouldn't be able to sleep until it was on paper and out of my head, but I hadn't expected him to wake up while I was working on it. I had thought I would be able to take it home and work on it all day and get it perfect.

I was almost holding my breath as I waited for Lo to react or say something and almost lost my nerve all together waiting for him to respond.

"It's really nothing special, if you don't like it that's ok." I said reaching for the sketchpad. "Like I said I just needed to get it down so I could sleep."

Lo pulled the drawing away from me before I could grab it from him, holding up a hand to stop me. He levered himself up in the bed so he was sitting with his back against the headboard. He still hadn't looked at me but I could see his eyes taking in every detail of the drawing.

I watched his hand as he touched the ragged and battered wings then trace the line of the chain of the dog tags. The soldier's face was obscured by his head bowed, his forehead resting on the hand holding the tags.

Finally Lo looked up at me and I saw tears shimmering in his eyes.

He took a deep ragged breath and cleared his throat then rubbed the heels of his hands into his eyes.

"Thank you." He said letting out a shaky breath. "This is so perfectly amazing. Are you going to colour it? You said red and white poppies, but right now they're pencil."

"I don't know." I shrugged, finally relaxing knowing he didn't hate it. "Um, I thought the soldier would be shaded in grays and blacks and kind of left as a rough sketch, but the wings would be open and glowing almost, bright yellows and oranges, almost like flames. And of course the poppies I think will be blood red. It only seems fitting given the amount of blood spilled on the battlefield."

"Fuck baby, it's perfect." He turned and set the drawing on the nightstand against the lamp so it was standing like a framed picture. "Come here." He held his arms out to me, inviting me to settle against his chest. "Did you mean for that to be our MC patch?"

"It occurred to me yes, but really Lo, it's yours to do with what you want." I whispered, kissing his chest.

"It's going on my back Alana, colour and all." He kissed the top of my head and squeezed my shoulders then whipped his t-shirt off of me. "Now that I've got you naked you can show me your ink baby." He smirked at me, swatting my ass. I squeaked and jumped off the bed.

"Ok," I chuckled, standing in front of him with my arms akimbo. "The first three are easy, the maple leaf in the volleyball," I pointed at my right hip, "volleyball got me through high school. The stylized crucifix," I pointed to my left hip, "Jesus gets me through life. The Celtic cross on my lower back," I turned, pointing to my back, "got a bit of Scots in me. And the piece de resistance," I chuckled pulling my hair over my shoulder and revealing the tattoo on my upper back.

"Fuck babe, that's beautiful, did you draw it?" Lo rose up on his knees and traced the lines of my tattoo with his rough fingertip. "What does it all mean?"

"Hmm, it's me and my boys." I answered smiling at him over my shoulder. "The bamboo is because all of my boys' names mean strength of some sort; they all have two middle names. Each flower is for their birth months, rose for June, iris for February, narcissus for December, larkspur for July and daisy for April. Around the bamboo is twined ivy for fidelity and then the mother holding the child and the semi-colon for the battle against mental illness." I gasped as both Los hands bracketed my waist and his warm mouth kissed each flower on my back.

"What's written in the bamboo?" He asked quietly, licking the length of the words.

"*Auxilium meum a domino.*" I whispered as he kissed higher up my back and his big hands smoothed up my stomach to cup my breasts. "The Lord is my salvation."

Lo kissed and sucked and licked up my neck still exposed from when I moved my hair over my shoulder. He bit the curve of my neck where it met my shoulder and I gasped again.

"I'm gonna take you like this baby." He whispered, sucking my earlobe into his mouth. "Are you ready? Should I fuck you from behind like this?"

"Yes," I breathed, "Please Lo, fuck me, I need you."

"You're beautiful Alana, your ink is beautiful and your amazing silky skin. I love the feel of you against me. You're so soft, everywhere I'm so hard. You fit against me so perfectly." He said as he trailed one hand down to my soaking pussy and the other tweaked first one and then the other nipple, alternating between massaging my breasts and pinching my nipples. "Spread your legs baby, let me in. You're going to come on my hand first, and then I'm going to drive my cock in to you and fuck you until you scream."

"Lo." I moaned, already primed just from his words.

His fingers stroked my clit then delved into my wet hole, spreading my juices all over me. He worked me, his fingers pushing into me then pulling out and flicking my clit. First hard then feather light, until I felt my inner muscles clench and my back bowed and I rested my head back on his shoulder.

"Lo . . ." I whispered as I slowly came down from my orgasm and he skimmed his hand up my stomach, rubbing my wetness into me as he went. The heat from his chest left my back for a split second before he was pulling me back with him onto the bed.

"Come here baby, sit on my legs." He whispered, pulling me back and spreading my thighs so he fit between them, pulling my arms up to clasp behind his head.

He held my hips and drove into me from behind, making me cry out then wrapped one arm around my hips holding me in place and placed his other hand on my chest at the base of my throat.

He moaned behind me as he pulled out slowly and surged back in quickly. Lo kept his pace for a few pumps until I moaned and leaned my head back on his shoulder, turning to take his mouth in a hot, wet kiss.

Finally Lo sped his pace, pumping hard and fast into me making my breasts jump with every thrust. The arm around my waist slid up to hold my breasts and the other came up to hold under my jaw, keeping my head back giving him better access to suck and nip at my throat.

"Oh fuck, Lo . . . I'm coming . . . please baby, make me come." His hand around my throat slid down between my legs and pinched my clit and I clenched and came on a scream. Lo pumped twice more before grunting and coming on a roar as I felt his hot cum fill me up.

Afterwards we sat on the bed panting for a long while catching our breaths. I slumped back against him feeling so wrung out, feeling him slide out of me.

"Lo, I think you broke me," I moaned when he tried to lay us down. "I don't think I can move." He chuckled as he got comfortable then pulled me back against him and wrapped his arms around me tighter.

"Sleep baby, it's not even 5 in the morning. What time you gotta be home?" Lo asked, brushing my hair off my forehead.

"Not early, I went to church with the boys and mom and dad last night and they said they'd call before they brought the boys home. I told them I planned on sleeping in and then cleaning and writing the rest of the day." I whispered, snuggling back into him and hugging his arm tight against my chest. "My mother loved that. If she thinks I'm cleaning she'll probably keep the boys until bedtime tonight." Lo snorted behind me and kissed my shoulder.

"Sleep babe, I'll go back to your place with you tomorrow afternoon and help you clean."

"It's clean, Lo. My mom is just a little OCD." I giggled thinking about my mom and how wonderful she was. "I suppose you're going to have to meet my parents."

"Ok."

"You're not going to freak out about meeting my parents?" I asked, rolling onto my stomach to look at him.

"No babe, parents are easy, it's your kids I'm worried about meeting. Now go to sleep, nothing's happening at five in the morning."

"Ok Lo." I said and snuggled into his chest with my nose tucked into his neck.

CHAPTER 15

Lo

When I woke up a few hours later Alana was still tucked in against my chest. If I didn't have to piss so bad I would've woken her up and fucked her again. I turned over and looked again at the drawing she did of the soldier and felt myself choking up again.

I looked at the clock and saw it was 10 and decided to get out of bed. I went to the bathroom then got dressed and headed to the kitchen for some coffee. Hammer was there when I walked in drinking his own cup of coffee.

"Hammer," I nodded to him. "How's your throat?" He held out his hand palm down and tipped it from side to side. "So-so, when's your doctor's appointment?"

Tuesday, he signed then shrugged.

"I'm gonna hit the gym, you wanna come with? Spot me and I'll return the favour?" Hammer sent a chin lift my way and we left the kitchen. I didn't get much time lately to work out and even after last night with Alana I had a lot of extra energy that I needed to expend.

Hammer and I worked well together, especially when he wasn't talking and I needed time to think. We still needed to get this code of Demon's figured out, when I was done here I decided I would check with Seether and see how things were progressing there.

With that decision made I let my wander and random thoughts float in and out of my head while Hammer and I worked out. Eventually Seether and Axle came in and started their own work-out, turning on the death metal Seether preferred to listen to. Personally it made me cringe but, to each his own right?

Invariably when my mind wandered I ended up thinking of the MC and everything we had accomplished in the last five years. We weren't a typical MC; we didn't have church like so many MCs did.

We didn't have huge meeting rooms where we left our cell phones outside and every member swore an oath of secrecy. We were just a bunch of guys looking out for each other who came home from a terrible experience broken and needing a brotherhood.

Our ol' ladies were just girlfriends and wives and we didn't run anything illegal. Not money laundering, not drugs, not guns and definitely not pussy. We were all ex-military and believed in law and order and freedom and rights.

We went to horrible places in the world and fought for those very things. We certainly were not going to come home and take those things from people in our own country.

Because we all had backgrounds in the military we all had per-mits to own handguns and once in a while we went hunting. Often we would carry rifles when we worked on the ranch in case a coyote thought one of our horses would make a tasty snack.

We were all more comfortable being armed than not, but legally just owning the weapons had to be enough. We didn't believe in hiding from the police and believed in full disclosure. It was rare that officers came to the club house thinking we were trouble but we had far too much respect for our brothers and sisters in blue.

More often than not we worked side by side with the police in town. We were all trained in first aid and were all trained in search and rescue and volunteered whenever we were needed. We had a large portion of the earnings from our companies go towards local charities and every year we had a charity ride.

As much as it all helped our community it also helped each of us. We needed to feel needed and necessary. We needed to be able to go out into the community and be proactive. It also helped when a guy was deep in therapy and needed to test the waters of going out in public and not freaking out or having a PTSD episode.

I was pulled from my musings when I heard Hammer start to cough. Since his throat was so sore lately he'd been taking it easier. I thought nothing of him coughing until he dropped down from the bar he was doing pull ups on and bent at the waist.

He coughed harder for a few minutes then spit what looked like blood onto the floor. He started to stand up but seemed to get dizzy and dropped to one knee, throwing out a hand to brace himself on the stands of the pull up bar.

We all rushed to him when we saw the blood but he waved us off, saying he was fine but when he tried to take another deep breath his eyes rolled back in his head and he fell back against the wall.

"Hammer!"

CHAPTER 16

Alana

When I woke up the bed was empty. I wasn't really surprised, but it was still warm so Lo couldn't have been gone that long. I looked over at the clock on his night stand and saw the green glow showing 11:45. I stretched and smiled up at the ceiling then rolled out of bed and went to shower.

I washed quickly then got dressed and applied a little mascara but left my hair wet hanging down my back. I pulled Lo's t-shirt from last night on again even though I had brought a change of clothes and the pair of shorts I had brought and went to find him.

I found the kitchen easy enough from the smell of coffee but found the space empty. I poured myself a cup and left the kitchen to explore. I was just walking into the main room when one of the guys I had met the night before came in the front door.

"You looking for Prez?" he asked, seeing I was looking lost, I think his name was Needles but I couldn't remember everyone I had met last night. He was covered in tattoos though and I think I would remember that.

I nodded and smiled and he pointed me to the gym. A gym? Shit, Lo was probably going to make me work out now. I was just stepping into the room to see Lo, Axle and Seether gathered around Hammer as he fell back against the wall.

"Hammer!" Lo yelled, reaching out to grab the other man.

"What the fuck!" Axle exclaimed as the three of them laid Hammer on the floor.

"Lo!" I cried, rushing over to them, "What happened?"

"We don't know babe." Lo said crouching over his friend. "His throat's been bugging him, he just coughed up a bunch of blood then passed out. Hammer, wake up man." Lo slapped Hammer's cheeks lightly trying to get him to open his eyes. Slowly his lids fluttered and he groaned.

Hammer's hands met over his chest and slowly he signed *help* and *hurts to breath.*

"Let's go man, let's get you to the hospital." Axle helped pull Hammer to his feet and he and Seether helped support Hammer out of the room.

"I'm sorry babe," Lo said, pulling me into a hug. "I wanted to spend the day with you but I gotta get Hammer to the hospital."

"It's ok Lo," I replied rubbing his back. "You need to see to Hammer, he's more important right now. Call me later and let me know how he's doing. I'll just go home and work on that drawing and all that cleaning my mother thinks I need to do." He snorted but smiled a little.

"You're amazing, babe. I'll call you later." And with that he was gone to look after his brother. I grabbed my stuff from his room and made my way home. I stopped to get a coffee and saw the strangest girl at the Esquires.

She was really very lovely, driving the hottest car I had ever seen. My dad would be so jealous of her '69 electric blue mustang. The back of her t-shirt was torn in strips and tied back together exposing the cutest cat paw print tattoo marching up her spine. Her hair was a bright green with blue streaks.

When she climbed into her car I noticed it had Ontario license plates on it and I wondered if she was driving through or if she had just moved to town. As I watched her she pulled big rockabilly sunglasses over her eyes and started her car. It roared to life and she looked over her shoulder to pull out of her parking spot. She saw me smiling at her and smiled back waving her fingers then drove away.

I took my coffee from the barista and drove home. I did a quick check of the house to make sure everything was mostly clean if not tidy and sat at my desk in my office with my sketch pad. I had work to do and I wanted to get the drawing finished before I saw Lo again.

I don't know how long I sat there drawing and colouring and shading but I'm pretty sure once I sat down I didn't move until I heard the doorbell ring. I looked at my watch and saw it was three in the afternoon. Excellent, I had been sitting in the same position for almost three hours. I knew it couldn't be my parents with my kids; they wouldn't ring the bell so I figured I should probably answer it.

I jumped up and immediately regretted the quick movement. My back had seized, just great. Slowly I made my way down the stairs to the front door stretching the muscles in my back as I went. By the time I got to the door and had it open Lo had his fist raised to knock.

"Hey," I said smiling at him, pushing at the muscles in my lower back.

"You all right babe?" He frowned at me massaging my lower back.

"Yeah," I laughed, "I was just sitting in the same position for about two hours; my back is a little stiff. Come in." I held the door wide for him to step inside then left it open to let a breeze in. "How's Hammer?"

"Don't know babe." Lo sighed, shoving his hands through his still wet hair. "He made us leave him at the hospital. When we left he was waiting for a CT scan or something." I lifted a hand to touch his waist while I placed my other hand on his jaw, rubbing his bottom lip with my thumb.

"Does this happen often, Lo?"

"Not since he came home as far as I know. His mom said when she first called me to see if I would take him in that his throat was in bad shape, but the drugs he was taking for the pain was making it worse. Now he refuses to take even an Advil." Lo said as he gently pushed a hand into my hair at the side of my head.

"He's a recovering addict." I stated.

"Yup, but that's his story." Lo replied then kissed me softly on the lips. "How's the house cleaning going?"

"It would be going a lot better if she wasn't attached to you at the moment." I snorted and looked over Lo's shoulder to see my mother standing in the open front door with her arms full of shopping bags. "Your boys needed new clothes so we went to the mall." She said when I looked pointedly at the bags.

"They did not mom." I rolled my eyes at the bags, "You were played again."

"I can only be played if I didn't know better." She said whisking past us and up the stairs. Before she got to the top a throat cleared behind us. We turned to see my dad standing in the door with my boys and Chelle.

Mom's got a boyfriend! Drew signed gleefully.

Get out of here you meathead! I signed and translated then ruffled his hair then sent him upstairs to help his grandmother.

"Lo," I sighed, and then took a deep breath trying to prepare myself for the shit show that was meeting my family. "Lo, this is my dad, Darren and my boys Nate, Cal, Jack and Link. Guys, this is Logan Winters."

"It's a pleasure to meet you, sir." Lo said politely holding his hand out to my dad, "Alana has told me quite a bit about you." My dad grunted at him and looked down at the hand extended to him. Just as I was about to admonish him for being rude my dad took Lo's hand and shook it firmly.

"Alana's boys have been telling us about you this weekend." My dad said looking Lo in the eye. My dad was a good five inches shorter than Lo but that didn't stop him from seeming bigger than life. "They've had good things to say."

"I'm glad to hear that, sir. I haven't had time to really meet and spend time with the boys yet, Alana's asked we go slowly; she doesn't want anyone getting attached if things don't work. I agreed with her at first, but now I'm not so sure."

"Meaning?" My dad demanded as I frowned at Lo.

"Meaning sir, I love your daughter. I'm not letting her go and honestly I'm more worried about me getting attached to her boys and them not liking me than them getting attached to me and me leaving." Lo shrugged as though he was talking about the weather, when the magnitude of what he just said was potentially earth shattering. After what seemed like forever with time standing still as Lo and my dad stared at each other, dad finally nodded his head.

"Well Logan, I can see from the look in your eyes you're serious and you're not dickin' around-"

"Darren Hun, stop swearing in front of the kids and go outside to threaten Logan's manhood." My mother said as she breezed down the stairs and then out of the room into the kitchen. "Boys, go put your new clothes away while I talk to your mom."

"Yes Grandma!" They all said at once and disappeared up the

stairs and I heard one of them snicker and say something like 'moms in trouble now.' Little brats! Here I was raising a village but apparently I was the village idiot.

"Come on Logan," my dad said, snickering himself, "Let's go have a beer on the deck." My dad walked past me and through the kitchen stopped at the fridge and grabbed a couple of bottles of beer then kissed my mom on the cheek and continued out to the deck. I looked back at Logan completely dumbfounded and he just smiled at me.

"Told you parents were easy babe." He said, kissing my lips lightly and swatting my ass then following my dad out. As he went he stopped in the kitchen and formally introduced himself to my mother and complimented her on something or other then proceeded out to the deck with my dad.

"Alana!" my mother called when I didn't immediately join her in the kitchen.

"Coming," I mumbled.

CHAPTER 17

Lo

Spending the afternoon with Alana and her family was far from a hardship. Her dad had a very stern discussion with me, or rather he had one at me while I listened and nodded my agreement. And he was right, I was seriously considering taking on not just a woman, but her kids, six of them. I had a second of panic when that really hit me and I thought about it, but then I stopped and realized Alana's kids were nothing to worry about.

At one point Darren looked at me seriously and told me I would screw up, and shit would hit the fan, and that was ok. He said he knew that because he had been married to Joann for almost 50 years and he was still screwing up. It's what men did he said, our women expected it just as long as we didn't screw up too badly we would be fine.

That was his advice, don't screw up too badly cause he wasn't the one I had to worry about. Alana's brother was at least as big as me and he had some pretty serious anger management issues Darren said, and the brother didn't fight fair, anything was fair game. Baseball bats, golf clubs, whatever he could find if he heard that I had hurt his sister. Oddly enough that made me pretty happy to hear that. If he couldn't look out for Alana then he knew someone would.

After that Alana's mom Joann, who was vegetarian, made Darren start up the grill and make the rest of us burgers while she fried her own veggie thing in a pan. Alana, her boys and her parents had a very tight knit vibe and I loved watching them interact with each other.

The only thing missing was Michelle. Joann said Michelle had chosen to stay at their house when they said they were bringing the boys home. Joann said Michelle had been completely engrossed in some piece of art she was working on and hated to have her groove interrupted so Joann left her to it.

Darren and Joann were just getting ready to leave for the evening, the dishes were done, the boys were fed and happy, and just getting ready for bed when I got a text from Axle.

Hammer's home.

Reading it made me sigh deeply and draw and glance from Darren. I shot back a quick answer and put my phone back in my pocket.

"Everything alright Logan?" He asked lightly, giving me the chance to say it was fine and leave it alone.

"I don't know Darren." I replied instead. "We had to rush one of my guys to the hospital today. His larynx is damaged and he's been having trouble the last couple of weeks with pain. We don't know if he overdid it today or if it's something more serious but he started coughing up blood while we were working out."

"You're worried." He stated the obvious. "Joann's nephew is a nurse at the hospital, ask Alana to reach out to him for help. I'm sure he'll be happy to."

"Thanks Darren," I nodded, shaking the older man's hand.

"Remember what I said earlier, don't screw up too badly. My son doesn't like leaving home if he doesn't have to, adds to his anger issues, don't make me call him to come and kill you." Darren clapped me on the shoulder and left Alana's house. Joann hugged Alana and followed Darren out into the dark evening.

"What was that about?" Alana asked, fitting herself under my arm and wrapping hers around my waist.

"Your dad was just threatening to call you brother to kill me if I screwed up too badly."

"Ah, you should take that to heart. It's not an idle threat and you wouldn't be the first." She smirked and ran up the stairs to say good night to her boys. When she came back down I had tossed myself on the couch and was fiddling with my phone, willing Hammer to send me a message.

"So," Alana said, coming back into the living room with two bottles of beer in her hands. She handed me one and sat beside me, curling her legs under her and resting her knees on my thigh. "About what you told my dad earlier tonight . . . "

"Which part baby?" I looked at her expectantly. A lot had been said tonight but I was pretty sure I knew what she meant.

"Oh you know, the part where you told my dad you loved me and you were worried about my kids not liking you. And the part where you decided rather arbitrarily that you were done taking things slowly."

"All truth baby. I don't know your kids well yet but from the little time I spent with them this afternoon I know they're amazing and you're an awesome mom. I know I want to know them more. I am worried that they won't like me but I will work hard every day for them to see that I will take care of them and I will do everything I can to make them understand I will do anything and everything for them and their mom."

"Lo-, " I held up my hand and stopped her.

"I know we still need to take things slowly. I know that and I'm fine with it. I know that I'm not just going to up and move in tomorrow, or next month or even a year from now. I know that even though you and I will progress in our relationship kids don't work the same way adults do. I know that would be a lot for them to handle, especially the older boys who remember and miss their dad.

"I get it, but you get this, I love you and I am going to marry you one day. I want you in my life and in my arms. You've already taken residence in my heart and I'm not letting you go." When I finally finished my mini tirade Alana just stared at me, then leaned forward and pressed her lips to mine.

"I love you Logan Winters."

It was a week later and the guys and I were all busy getting the club house ready for the family bbq. All the guys who had kids were bringing them for the party and Alana had invited her parents and her friend Brooke. Michelle had agreed to come as well even though she was still apprehensive about the club and the guys in it.

Hammer had come home from the hospital the week before and gone straight to his room to stay and hadn't come out except to work. His doctor's appointment on Tuesday didn't go well either if his mood the last few days was any indication.

I had met Alana's cousin the nurse Thursday afternoon to pick his brain about what Hammer might be going through and he was actually very helpful, especially since Hammer wasn't telling us anything.

To say I was surprised meeting the cousin is an understatement. The dude was huge. I was expecting an average guy, average height, average looks, average everything. What I got was a guy far from average. If the looks the other nurses were shooting him were any indication the guy was hot and none of them cared that his wedding ring was on display, or that his wife the psychologist joined us for lunch.

Alana's cousin Iain might have been soft spoken, but he was smart and compassionate. He was easily as tall as me but built more like Seether but still pretty heavily muscled. When I asked Alana about Iain she laughed and said she could remember when they were kids and Iain would eat six plates of spaghetti and twelve hot dogs and still be hungry.

She said he grew so fast his muscles and circulation couldn't keep up and he often had fainting spells. In high school he broke every track, volleyball and basketball record in the school and his son was following closely in his dad's footsteps, including his size.

I was glad I had met with Iain, even though the information he gave me was less than heartening. I decided to give Hammer until Sunday afternoon to tell me what the hell was going on and then I was going to drag him out of his room and drown him in beer if I had to.

I looked up at a noise from inside the club house and saw Alana et al come through the back door into the yard. Even Drew was making a ton of noise. Alana bee-lined to me and grabbed me around the shoulders, laying a hot kiss on my mouth.

"I missed you." She whispered, licking my bottom lip. I chuckled at her and patted her ass then hugged her tight. It had been a crazy busy week for her with the end of school so we hadn't seen much of each other. She had finished my tattoo by Monday and had delivered it to me but I had been out.

I had a surprise for her, though. I had gotten with our regular artist and had him put it on my back. It was probably much bigger than she had planned it to be considering it covered my back across my shoulder blades and down to the waistband of my jeans but I didn't care, I loved it.

"Mom and dad are taking the boys home with them after the bbq, I'm free for as long as you want me."

"Forever? Yup, forever works." I mumbled against her lips and kissed her again.

"How's Hammer?" She asked, pulling away from me when Axle stepped up to us with a couple of beers.

"Hey Alana," He said before I could answer her question. "Your kids are awesome. Those two middle ones, they play sports?"

"Cal and Jack? Yeah, you name it they play it. Cal is actually a curling superstar, but he loves baseball in the summer and a bit of soccer. He plays volleyball and basketball at school and he runs long distance with the school running club."

"Which one is he?" Axle asked, watching my boys chase each other through the yard.

"Cal is the older of the two. Jack is the one with the ball right now; he's a little bit smaller than Cal, but not for long. He's a soccer star. He'll play other stuff but soccer is his love, soccer and math." She grimaced, like the word math left a bad taste in her mouth.

"How about the oldest?" Seether asked walking up on my other side. "What's his name?"

"That's Nate. He's the artist and apparently the carpenter. Then number four is Link and no, that's not short for Lincoln, it's just Link. My husband was tired of normal names by the time Link came along. Link is just fast. He's only nine but he already runs faster than all three of his older brothers. He's pretty mellow, too. Not much gets him excited."

"The youngest Drew is hilarious." I told the guys. "When he gets excited and can't talk fast enough he starts signing and I swear I need an interpreter. But the stuff that comes out of that kid's mouth is insane." All the guys chuckled with me as we watched the kids play with the members' kids.

Darren and Joann sat off to the side with bottles of water talking to Sharpie and his wife. It looked like everyone was having a good time. It didn't take long before Drew broke away from the other kids waving his hand in the sign for potty then disappeared into the clubhouse.

I hadn't noticed earlier but Brooke had come in with Alana and her family and was now sitting off to the side with Michelle. I kissed Alana on the side of her head and walked over to Michelle and Brooke. Brooke saw me coming and smiled and stood just as I reached them. She touched my arm on her way by as though I needed that fortifying touch.

"Mind if I sit?" I asked, standing over the girl. She looked up at me, pensive for a minute then smiled and moved to the side to give me room. "I'm really sorry about your dad."

"You don't beat around the bush do you?" She smirked, watching the kids playing.

"And you are much older than fourteen, I think you've had to grow up faster than your years." Michelle smiled and shrugged. "I'm more sorry that I wasn't paying enough attention when your dad needed me. I'm sorry I wasn't there for you when I should have been."

"It's not your fault my dad had his demons, you think that's where he got his name?"

I nodded, "Maybe, he had the name before I met him. He was a good man."

"I'll take your word for it." She snickered. "I don't doubt you mean it, or that you're right. You just knew him a whole lot better than I did. Still, I miss him."

"We all do." We watched the kids for a while before either of us spoke again. "Alana told you he wasn't doing anything illegal when he died, right? She told you he was tapped by the feds?"

"Yeah, she told me. Unfortunately that doesn't make him any less dead." She shrugged.

"True. Did Alana also tell you that he had set up a savings account for you? He'd been putting money in it for a long time, I think even before you came to live with him."

She shook her head angrily, "That's so stupid! I didn't know he existed or where he was and he made no effort to meet me or see me but he put money away for me? Was that a balm to his soul?"

"I don't know." I sighed, at a loss as to what to tell her. "Did your mom ever tell you why your dad wasn't a part of your life?"

"No, she just said he wasn't capable of being a dad or a husband. I think she knew where he was living, but made no effort to contact him."

"Look Michelle-"

"Chelle, I'm not that girl anymore."

"Ok. I love Alana and I'm going to marry her, hopefully soon. She already considers you her daughter and I would never do anything to hurt her. I promise you from now on I will take care of you like I will her boys. I hope you can accept that from me."

"Mr. Winters, I'm glad Mrs. M found you. I'm glad you love her and she loves you and you want to take care of her and the boys. I want that too for myself, but it will take me longer to accept it."

"Call me Lo, Chelle. I understand your apprehension and I promise I will work hard every day to prove to you that you can trust me. And once I have your trust I won't break it." I laid my hand palm up on my thigh and waited for her to take it if she wanted. Eventually she did but didn't look at me again. A few minutes later I heard Axle's voice raised and angry.

When I looked over to where he was standing he was looming over Brooke scowling at the much smaller woman. Brooke maybe reached the top of his breast bone but she wasn't backing down, though and there was no fear on her face.

She didn't look angry, just serene and tolerant, waiting for him to finish his tirade. When Axle was finished yelling in her face she smiled slightly, said something I couldn't understand and walked away.

"Looks like you've got other kids to worry about besides me." Chelle quipped beside me. I snorted and patted her hand then pulled her to me and kissed her forehead and stood to talk to Axle.

CHAPTER 18

Alana

"Alana, I'm going to head out." Brooke said stepping to my side. "I will call you next week, we'll do coffee."

"Sure Brooke, I hope you had a good time today." I hugged her and watched her go but before she got to the back door Axle stepped up to her and took her elbow.

"Where are you going, Angel?" He demanded.

"Home, David." She replied as though that were obvious.

"Why haven't you returned any of my texts or phone calls?"

"Because David, you and I are not friends, we are not dating and I told you we couldn't be more than acquaintances through mutual friends."

"Did that night mean nothing to you?" He whispered, crowding her and getting more in her face.

"That night was lovely David, but that doesn't change things. Now, I really do need to go." I watched as Brooke patted Axle on the chest and walked away. He was obviously mad but stood staring at the place Brooke had stood. The only outward sign of his anger was the crushed beer can in his hand.

"Uh, David?" Seether snickered at Axle.

"Fuck you asshole." Axle muttered, flipping Seether the bird and stomping away to get another beer.

"What was that about?" Lo asked, stopping behind me and wrapping his arms around me.

"No clue, apparently the two of them had a night that he thought was more special than she did. I didn't think they knew each other beyond meeting at the coffee shop two weeks ago."

Lo shrugged, "Got me."

"How's Chelle doing? You talked to her about her dad?" Before Lo could answer me Drew called to me from the door of the clubhouse. When I looked over it was to find him standing with Hammer holding the big man's hand in his.

"Look who I found!" the little boy called, "He knows sign! He can talk to me!"

"That's great Drew." I said smiling as he pulled Hammer across the yard to us. When the two of them stopped in front of us Drew's hands started moving a mile a minute. "Drew, slow down."

Mama! He signed, *this is Hammer, he hears but he can't talk. He rides a motorbike! He's gonna show me how!*

Is he? I asked out loud while I signed, smirking at Drew's new best friend. *That's good to know, Hammer.*

Hammer shook his head, sighing and signed, *It's not a big deal.*

It is to Drew. I replied smiling at Lo's friend, "How are you feeling?" Hammer shrugged and looked away.

Got bad news, just not ready to talk about it yet, he replied.

"You have until tomorrow afternoon." Lo told him sternly. "Then I'm gonna drag your ass out of your room and water board you if I have to until you tell me."

Hammer smirked again, *Deal.*

The rest of the day went quietly. After talking to Hammer, Drew dragged him away to a corner of the yard to converse in sign language. Whatever they were talking about must've been pretty funny because Drew fell over laughing so hard more than once.

It wasn't long before shadows began to gather around the yard and little ones started dropping off to sleep. My mother came to me just before 9 and hugged me and said her and dad were taking the boys and Chelle home. I hugged each of my kids and smoothing Drew's hair from where his head rested on Hammer's shoulder, sound asleep.

Once everyone was gone and most of the cleanup was done Lo pulled me behind him to his room. As soon as we got there he wrapped me up in his arms and kissed me softly and sweetly. It didn't take long before our breathing became heavy and we were pulling each other's clothes off and our kisses became much more intense.

"I have a surprise for you." Lo whispered when I started pushing his t-shirt up over his chest. He stepped back from me and reached behind him and pulled his shirt off like guys do, fucking sexy.

He tossed the shirt and turned away from me, showing me his back. My breath caught in my throat when I saw what he had done. The kneeling, winged soldier I had drawn was tattooed there and it covered his whole back. The colours were vibrant and the tattered wings looked like flame and the poppies spilling from the helmet looked like flowing blood. It was just as I had drawn it, it was perfect.

"Lo, it's amazing!" I exclaimed, reaching out to graze the edges with my fingertips that still looked tender. "It's beautiful."

Lo turned to me and cupped my jaw in his hands. "Alana, you're beautiful, your art is beautiful. Our regular artist is a member, his name's Needles, you met him last week. He was in awe of your drawing. He was still raving about it the last time I saw him. He couldn't make it to the bbq tonight but he wants to meet with you and talk about your art."

"Lo," I whispered as he tipped my chin up and kissed me again, licking into my mouth. I lifted my hands and buried them in his thick, soft hair. "Turn around." I said, pushing away from him slightly. He did as I asked and stood watching me over his shoulder. I leaned down and gently kissed the soldier on his back and he sucked in a sharp breath. "Does it still hurt?"

"No." He rasped as the muscles in his back quivered from my touch. I trailed my lips slowly along the wings across his shoulders and skimmed my hands down his sides.

I placed one hand on his rippled stomach and held him in place while I kissed down his back sinking to my knees, then licked along the waistband of his jeans. I pulled on the belt loops of his jeans and turned him slowly to face me then kissed his belly button, licking inside as I undid the button and zipper of his jeans.

"Babe . . ."

"Shhh," I calmed him and I pushed his jeans and boxer briefs down his hips. His huge, hard, hot cock popped out of his underwear and seemed to wave at me. Before he could stop me I wrapped my hand around the base of him and licked the head. He moaned as a drop of pre-cum seeped out onto my tongue.

"Babe . . . you don't need to . . ." He whispered, trying again to tell me it's not necessary for me to do this for him. His cock was so hard and so big but covered in satiny smooth skin. The veins thick and bulging, his dick was beautiful.

"I want to," I whispered back, licking the underside of him from the base to the tip. "Let me love you, Lo." I said then took him into my mouth and sucked him as deep as I could, rubbing my saliva over him with my hand.

He moaned again, burying his hands gently into my hair, not to control or over power but to steady me. I moaned with him as I tasted more of him and he pulled back but I grabbed his ass with my free hand, holding him to me.

After a few minutes of me bobbing up and down and licking then sucking his balls into his mouth, Lo pulled back harder and lifted me off my knees.

"Baby I don't want to come in your mouth." He whispered, sipping at my lips.

He pulled my shirt off me and undid the button and zipper of my shorts, pushing them down my legs then cupping my pussy through my underwear.

"You're so fucking wet, your panties are soaked. Does sucking my dick get you off baby?"

"Lo, all of you gets me off. Your dick is just one more thing I like to put in my mouth."

CHAPTER 19

Lo

"Fuck baby, you're so fucking hot. You keep up that kind of talk and I'm gonna blow before I even get inside you." I groaned as I petted her through her underwear with one hand and undoing the clasp of her bra with the other.

She whimpered when I pulled my hand from between her legs to pull her panties off, kneeling in front of her to help her step out of them and the shorts piled around her ankles. "Lo, I need you inside me."

"You'll get me, but I gotta taste you first." I said then licked from her entrance up to her clit. She gasped and cried out, pushing her pussy against my mouth, begging for more. "Spread your legs more, baby."

She did as I asked and I sunk my tongue into her heat and licked her inner walls. She shrieked and grabbed handfuls of my hair, holding me against her, like I would move away before I was finished eating her.

She started to shiver and twitch as I lapped at her, spreading her juices from her entrance to her clit then pushed a finger inside her. I pulled my finger out and she moaned but started panting harder as I spread her wetness back to her ass hole and pushed on the tight rose.

"Anyone ever had you here, baby?" I asked her, kissing up her stomach.

She shook her head hard and whispered, "No."

"Do you want me to fuck your ass?"

"No, Lo. I don't want that," I took my hand from her and stood, looking down at her, I would not push her for something she wasn't comfortable with. "I like playing there Lo, but not full penetration."

"It's ok baby, I don't need it, and if you don't want it then neither do I." I kissed her hard letting her taste herself on my tongue as I pushed her back against the bed and lowered her to loom over her.

I pulled her knee up around my waist and slowly pushed into her. I kissed her, my tongue mimicking what I was doing with my dick inside her pussy. Quickly she started to whimper and writhe beneath me until she had to pull her mouth from mine and arch her neck, pushing her head back into the bed.

She cried out again as the walls of her pussy gripped my cock and strangled me so hard I couldn't hold on any longer and came so hard inside her. I slammed myself into her once more and she pulled both her knees up around my waist, trying to pull me deeper into her. I moved against her, grinding my pelvis against her clit and she arched again, screaming my name.

"Fucking heaven baby," I said when I could finally talk. "Holding you and being inside you is like heaven. You know that Nickelback song? I think it's called Holding onto Heaven? That's this right here baby. I love you with everything that I am. You're going to marry me soon."

"Ok Lo," she whispered, sinking her nose into my neck. "When you ask properly I'll answer properly, but for now you broke me."

I smirked at her, "Ok baby."

"You'll have to play that song for me later." She said and dropped off to sleep. I rolled onto my side and pulled her into me, holding her tight. Lying on my back to sleep was still tough with my tattoo but as long as I could hold her it didn't matter. I kissed her forehead and let myself follow her into sleep.

It was lunch time the next day before we all stumbled out of our rooms. Alana was sitting on my lap whispering in my ear when Hammer sat at the table with us. I looked over to him and waited for him to start. We would've been there all day if I didn't give in.

"What's going on Hammer?"

He sighed and lifted his hands to sign, *Waiting for the other guys, only wanna do this once.*

Axle walked into the room just as Hammer finished and turned back to holler for Seether to get his ass to the main room. Once all the guys were sitting comfortably and we all had our coffee cups full Hammer started.

You know when my convoy hit that IED I injured my voice box and after that I sunk pretty low. He paused, rubbing his hands over his face in frustration and almost hopelessness. *When I first came back the doctors had to take out a good portion of the cartilage that makes up my voice box. That's why I can't talk loudly, the larynx doesn't make sound, it regulates pitch and volume.*

Lately mine has been so sore it felt like I was swallowing glass. That day in the gym I couldn't get a deep breath, I felt like I was choking and then when I did catch my breath the air made me choke more and cough. I passed out from lack of oxygen to my brain.

Hammer stopped signing and pushed his chair back and put his elbows on his knees then dropped his head into his hands. I could tell he was on the verge of tears but I didn't know what to do for him but wait. Finally he sat up again and brushed the tears from his cheeks that he had let fall.

In the ER that day the doctor did a couple of scans. Normally they'd have done a swab and left it at that but because of my previous injury they wanted to be extra careful. They forwarded the results of the scans to my regular doctor and Tuesday at my appointment he said what was left of my larynx would have to be removed along with a good sized tumor. They think it might be cancerous but they won't know for sure until they do a biopsy.

"Fuck brother!" Axle exclaimed, shoving his hands through his hair and slumping back in his chair.

Alana sniffled and wiped tears from her own cheeks and left my lap to kneel at Hammers side and hug him tight. When she pulled away she held his face in her hands and stared into his eyes, tears cascading down her face.

Thank you, he signed and hugged her again, burying his face in her shoulder.

His shoulders rose and fell as he took deep breaths, trying to control himself.

"Hammer, what do you need?" I asked, gripping my coffee cup.

He sat up and looked around the table at us then patted Alana's shoulder and motioned her back to me.

Don't know yet. I have another appointment to find out what all is included in this surgery, and what the plan is for after. Alana, Prez told me about your cousin in the ER and I got a hold of him. Even talked to his wife, she's a psychologist; she said she would help me work through all the shit in my head.

"That's good Hammer." Alana whispered sitting in my lap again and resting her head on my shoulder. We all sat quietly for a minute, lost in our own thoughts when the front door was thrown open with a bang making us all jump.

"Davy! Where the fuck are you?"

"Kat?" Axle answered the woman. "Is that you? What are you doing here?"

"It's her," Alana exclaimed, staring at the woman at the door dumbstruck. I stared at Alana like she was insane.

CHAPTER 20

Alana

"Her?" Lo demanded, "You know her?"

""Yes," I replied, "I mean no, I don't know her, I just saw her the other day. I was getting coffee last week when I left here and she was at the same coffee shop. She's rather eye catching, really nothing inconspicuous about her at all."

We watched as the girl walked over to our table, making a beeline straight for Axle.

"Kat, what are you doing here?"

"Looking for you of course, hence the reason I busted in here calling your name."

The girl shook her head and pulled her rockabilly glasses off her face and pushed them on top of her head. Her hair was the same as I remembered bright green with blue streaks and she was wearing tight jeans rolled at the cuff with chucks on her feet.

Axle let out a roar of frustration and rubbed his hands over his face, then tipped his head back, cocked his hip and put his hands on his waist and sighed.

"And just why were you looking for me, Kat?" He growled at her.

"Cat, the tattoo!" I smiled at the girl whose gaze snapped to mine.

"Yeah, but with a 'K', short for Katherine which I hate." She said squinting at me in concentration. "You look familiar."

I laughed, "I should, you caught me staring at you last week outside the Esquires. Nice car by the way."

"You brought the '69?" Axle demanded, turning to the door and stomping outside, yelling over his shoulder, "You drove my fucking mustang across the fucking country?"

Kat snorted as she watched him go then turned back to us. "I'm his sister by the way, nice to sort of meet you all."

"Sorry," I said stepping forward, "I'm Alana, Lo's girlfriend-"

"Fiancé." He interrupted me.

"Not until you ask properly." I snapped back.

"I remember Logan, from when he and Davy first came back from the forces, but he probably doesn't remember me." She said, looking at Lo expectantly. He held out his hand palm down and tipped it from side to side.

"I remember Axle saying he had a half-sister and his step dad was a prick, but I don't remember meeting you, sorry."

"No worries, there's fifteen years between us, I'm kind of forgettable, or at least I was at the time." She laughed, tugging a strand of her bright hair and shrugged then turned to Seether and Hammer. "And you gentlemen? You have names?"

"Seether." The man said holding his hand out to Kat as he stood from the table and smiling. "I'm gonna go back to my room, Hammer come find me when you're free. It was nice to meet you Kat." Kat smiled at Seether and watched him go then looked back at Hammer. He looked back at her and waited then sighed and gave in, losing the staring contest.

Hammer.

"What?" She demanded. Lo and I watched the exchange quietly, trying not to get involved but knowing we would probably have to help translate.

"He said his name is Hammer." I said smiling slightly.

"I know what he said, it just didn't make sense. Who the hell names their kid Hammer?"

It's my road name. He signed to her. *You know sign language?*

Yeah, she signed and spoke, *it comes in handy when people think you're stupid because you're dyslexic and can't read.* Hammer pushed out a breath that sounded like a 'huh' and nodded then signed sorry. "Don't be, I got over it."

It was at that moment that Axle pushed back into the club house and strode over to his sister, pulling her into his arms and hugging her tightly. He tucked his lips close to her ear and took a deep breath.

"Baby girl, what are you doing here?" He asked quietly, rocking her back and forth.

"Well," she replied, pulling back from her brother. "Shit hit the fan. Mom and dad are getting a divorce, I told dad I wanted to come and find you since it's been five or more years with no word from you, and dad got pissed and disowned me. Mom took off with a friend who I think is a woman but who knows, so I packed the '69, which is mine by the way, and left. And here I am."

"That car is mine."

"Possession being 9/10ths of the law and all makes it mine."

Axle rolled his eyes at her, "When did you get here?"

"Couple of weeks ago," She answered, shrugging. "I've been staying at a dive hotel and looking for a job but so far I haven't found anyone who wants a mechanic who can't read."

"Lo," Axle said looking at Logan.

"Done brother," Lo said, taking my hand. "We'll leave you to figure it out." He pulled me out of the room and Hammer followed us, going to his room.

When we made it to Lo's room he grabbed me around the waist and pulled me down on the bed with him then snuggled my back against his chest. We stayed that way for a few minutes, me running my fingers up and down Lo's arm and Lo playing with my hair.

"Alana," he suddenly said quietly, "Will you marry me?"

"Of course I will Lo." I answered, tipping my head to kiss his arm.

"You know when we get married we won't be able to live in the condo, right?" I nodded but didn't say anything. "You know there's a big house out back of the ranch? It needs a bit of work, and we've been using it for guys who needed to rehab but it's mostly empty now, just one guy left. If we fixed that up would you and the boys move in there?"

"Lo, I'm not moving in with you." I said, rolling over to look at him.

"No babe, I'm not asking you to move in with me. I'm asking you to move into my house until we get married. Then I'll move in with you, I'll stay here at the club house until we're married. You're too far away at the condo, and the house is paid for and it's way bigger. All the boys and Chelle will have their own rooms."

"Oh," I whispered, "It's about cost efficiency."

"If that's what it takes to get you to say yes." Lo said, swatting my ass and kissing me lightly on the lips.

"I think it's a great idea Lo, but let me talk to the boys and I'll let you know. Are you sure this is what you want?" I kissed him again then snuggled into his shoulder and closed my eyes.

"This is definitely what I want, forever thank you babe." I smiled, loving that he was thanking me for letting him take care of me and my kids.

It was months later and we were all back in the club house, we had just moved the kids and I into the ranch house and were taking a pizza break. The boys were with my parents getting school supplies since we were all back to school in a couple of days.

I hadn't seen Brooke since just after Lo asked us to move into his house. She wasn't answering my calls or texts and she had handed in her resignation at school. Axle was tight lipped about it and refused to talk about Brooke at all.

Kat was settling in well but even she couldn't get Axle to talk about Brooke. Kat had taken over another member's room when he had moved out to live with his fiancé and was working full time in the garage. The MC had been able to expand their business with her working for them into most custom classic car work and they were all happy about it.

Hammer's surgery had gone well enough, but he was still in a lot of pain and refusing to take medication for it. What was left of his larynx was removed along with the tumor that had been sitting on it. The biopsy had shown that the tumor was noncancerous but Hammer had to be checked for new cells and growths every few months.

Ever since his stay in the hospital he and Kat had formed a bond but no one knew why or how. We all just left it alone since Hammer was really good at ignoring people now that he couldn't talk and Kat could get prickly when she was feeling cornered.

We were in the clubhouse now waiting for her to join us for pizza when there was a commotion in the main yard. There were sounds of a scuffle and then Kat yelled "Hey!"

The main door banged open and Kat was held there by a man

standing behind her holding a gun to her head. She was standing at a strange angle because the man was holding her in place by her hair and she looked like she was on her toes trying to relieve the pressure on her scalp.

"What the fuck?" Axle roared, jumping up from his chair, sending it crashing to the floor.

"Stay right fucking there!" The man holding Kat yelled at Axle, moving the gun from her head to her brother. "Don't fucking move! You fuckers ruined my business, you've been warned, I'm going to ruin your fucking lives! I'm going to take everything from you!"

When he was done he raised his gun into the air and fired into the ceiling then pushed Kat away from him onto the floor. We all rushed forward to get to her, or at least tried since Lo pulled me behind him.

Hammer, Lo and Seether rushed out the door after the man but only caught a glimpse of the car he jumped into before it roared away. Axle and I helped Kat off the floor and made sure she wasn't hurt. He helped her sit at the table while I rushed to get her ice for her head.

"Are you ok?" He demanded.

"Who the fuck was that?" She snapped right back rubbing her scalp where her hair had been pulled.

"We don't know his name; we've been having problems with him for a few months now. We know he's a small time dealer and one of our guys got in the middle of his shit and got killed for it." Lo said as he and the other two guys came back into the room.

Hammer went straight to Kat, tucking his hand into the hair at the back of her head and touching his forehead to hers.

"I'm ok Sam." She whispered looking deep into his eyes and kissed him lightly on the lips. He shook his head and tapped his chest. "I know, I was scared, too but I'm ok."

We stood watching the exchange between the two then looked at each other flabbergasted. My gaze went straight to Axle but he shook his head at me.

"Don't look at me, this is news to me." He said gesturing to his sister and friend. Hammer sighed deeply and stepped back from Kat, holding her hand.

Sorry, he signed. *She wanted to wait to tell you.*

Axle pointed at him and held his gaze, "Don't make me kill you." Hammer smirked and nodded.

"I'm going to go to my office and call Sharpie, see if he knows anything more." Lo said, scratching the back of his head as he walked away.

"I'll come with you." Seether said nodding to Axle to follow. "I got some things to run past you guys."

"Fucking Demon," Axle exhaled as he followed Lo and Seether. "This all started with that shit head.

I looked around the now mostly empty room, "Well, I suppose I'll go finish unpacking."

The boys would be home any minute and I wanted to have at least most of their bedrooms ready for them. It was starting to look like our crazy run around lives just got crazier.

Printed in Great Britain
by Amazon

86191929R00068